D0407329

THEY SLEEP
WITHOUT
DREAMING

Also by Penelope Gilliatt

THEY SLEEP WITHOUT DREAMING

stories by

PENELOPE GILLIATT

Dodd, Mead & Company

NEW YORK

The following stories: "The Hinge," "The Wind-Child Factor," "Addio," "Broderie Anglaise," "Suspense Item," "Dame of the British Empire, BBC ," and "On Each Other's Time" originally appeared in *The New Yorker*. "The Nuisance" originally appeared in *Grand Street*. "They Sleep Without Dreaming" originally appeared in British *Vogue*. "Cliff-Dwellers" originally appeared in *The London Magazine*.

Copyright © 1982, 1983, 1984, 1985 by Penelope Gilliatt

All rights reserved

No part of this book may be reproduced in any form
without permission in writing from the publisher.

Published by Dodd, Mead & Company, Inc.
79 Madison Avenue, New York, N.Y. 10016
Distributed in Canada by
McClelland and Stewart Limited, Toronto
Manufactured in the United States of America

Designed by Claire Counihan

First Edition

Library of Congress Cataloging in Publication Data

Gilliatt, Penelope.
They sleep without dreaming.

I. Title.
PR6057.I58T48
1985   823'.914   85-7078
ISBN: 0-396-08493-1

CONTENTS

THEY SLEEP
WITHOUT
DREAMING

THE HINGE

T HEY FLEW IN VERY low over Warsaw. There was an
empty seat between Boleslaw and Wanda. They
tried, separately, to remember where they had
known each other before. No good. The empty seat, implying something; but for the moment nothing came back.
Two birds flying in flotilla on a level with the plane bumped
into each other.

"Birds in a migrating fleet don't usually bump," Wanda
said, in English.

"In a migration, there's bound to be dissent," said Boleslaw. The usual Polish double meaning: Polish Catholicism
standing also for anti-Soviet Communism, for instance.
Though he had been speaking German to the stewardess,
Boleslaw now used French, to fuddle the all too attentive
German-speaking Russians behind them. "Besides, they
can't be migrating. It's spring."

"De-migrating, then," she said, persisting in English. She

had seen him reading the label on a jar of Iranian caviar that he had shared with her. Another two birds bumped and their wings locked, being in cross-rhythm. "I didn't know birds syncopated," said Wanda.

"No. Any more than soldiers marching do. Except under order, on bridges."

"Why do you keep reading the label?"

"I'm not reading, I'm looking at Iranian," he said, in English. "Unintelligible and also illegible, with my eyesight. I broke my spectacles. A child with a swinging kit bag full of ironmongery did it at London Airport. At least, I would have deduced ironmongery. Saucepans and crowbars and spare kettle lids and such."

"A rising young tinker," she said. And then, "You *do* speak English, and also you don't look German at all."

"Why?"

"Why what?"

"In what way not?"

"You look like a Cruikshank. Big features. German features are more buried. And you've got a very non-German red beard." Another pair of birds bumped. "Sorry," said Wanda, apologising for something not her fault.

"So you are English, born and bred," he said. "All those 'Sorrys.'"

"No. Polish Jewish. English only since most of twenty-six years."

Something came back to Boleslaw for a second; the empty seat beside them filled up with some young ghost; but he still floundered. "Forget about it and it'll come back," people always said. So he left the question and held the caviar jar farther away from him to study the label, but Wanda saw no emergent clarity in his face and took the jar from him.

"They gave us Russian caviar with the lunch," she said.

He tried to hide the jar in his seat pocket with the safety instructions. " 'In the unlikely event of an emergency' in five languages," he said.

"Why didn't you have the Russian stuff?"

"Too greasy."

"Why does the Iranian jar matter?"

"Because it shows I've been in Iran, and my passport doesn't."

"You could have bought it in Soho. Either the caviar or the passport," she said after he had tried putting the empty jar into the instep of one of his socks. There is nowhere, nowhere at all, to hide an empty jar of Iranian caviar on plane or person when everything is going to be searched. He looked desperate. She leaned over him to whisper, and he said in a rush, obeying, "Soho, yes, of course—that's where you bought it."

Less calm than he about the likelihood of bugged headrests, she put her finger to her lips, and swiftly scratched off the Iranian label with her nail scissors and filled the jar half full of hair shampoo, so that she could carry in the evidence safely herself.

"I think the radar signals are messing up the birds' sense of direction," Boleslaw said.

She put her finger to her lips again, seeing another sort of trouble implicit for themselves, and studied his passport.

"A waiter," she said, seeing that he had altered "WRITER" to "WAITER," an easy enough change in the handwritten capitals of Her Britannic Majesty's passports. She flipped through the dozens of pages of visas. "You've been a waiter in a lot of countries," she said.

"At times. At *times,*" he said with emphasis.

Wanda nodded. Poles cotton on to codes quickly. All right, then, "WAITER" was a disguise for a correspondent of *The Times.*

"You must see a great deal of food, this way and that, in your profession," she said.

"Also a filmmaker and marionette-theatre director," he wrote inside the vapid human outline of a life-jacket diagram, and then he scratched over it and turned the writing into waiters' buttons and lapels. He whispered, "The Times' foreign bureau knows there isn't much to file safely from Poland." More loudly, "I am primarily an artist, you see, proud though I am of waitering, which serves our people."

"Where are you going now?" said Wanda, hands gripping the armrests as they came in to land. She added, in code again, "Official instructions: Is your headrest upright?"

"Near Lodz," he lied. "To do the washing-up at the film school." He inspected his headrest swiftly and found the mike stitched into a flabby violet in the antimacassar embroidery. "Possibly all washed up by now," he said.

She shook her head and said, "I expect the bumping—the bumping of birds—was a matter of de-migration. The captain of the flotilla giving the command to stay. No birds obeying. Communications among several thousand birds would be bound to be difficult. I believe it's colder this year in the Balkans than here. Nicer here, isn't it?" She screwed on the top of the hair-shampoo jar more tightly and then held his hand on the armrest, thinking not to clamour.

"So why are you coming back to Poland with a Polish birthplace on Her Britannic Majesty's passport?" He was only asking the immigration people's question for them. Pretending to be an upstanding line-toeing Pole. She approved the simulation.

"I've been working in a Polish bookshop in London and I got homesick," she said.

"To come would be risky, though?"

"No more than most things?"

"Because of the birthplace in your passport, as I said."

"A lot of regimes since then," she said.

"Bureaucrats are unchangeable."

"But stupid."

"Stupid and worldly. The most dangerous combination."

The plane in front of theirs suddenly changed course to the military side of the airport and crashed into a row of small government houses. When they landed, Boleslaw stayed seated. Wanda rushed to the accident. No one, it seemed from the first quick count, had been killed, even though the houses were made of matchstick. The passengers on the plane were Olympic athletes and their non-Polish coaches.

Sabotage was suspected. In a country of peril to everyone, from steelworkers to sandwich-makers, athletes had become to the outside world an emblem of the valuable: rare in constancy, running or swimming or pole-vaulting as they did, wrapped in the flag of their benighted nation.

Because Wanda had witnessed the accident, running in espadrilles from the plane to see what might be done, she was held at the airport for five hours. No one cared about what she was bringing in, apart from anything made of gold. Her rings (two) were taken off and counted again and again, and entered again and again on a form that had to be clipped to her exit form. Her earrings (also two, the one-per-head punk mode not yet having entered Poland) were also carefully counted and entered. A tooth of hers had recently been broken in London by a child on a skateboard. The dentist had covered the remaining witch's fang with a crown, which he felt might well come out again in a piece of Polish black bread, and he had therefore honourably supplied her with the jaw impressions he had taken, to save her possible expense of zlotys. The impressions looked to her Neanderthal, and also breakable.

"A zoologist," said one inspector.

"An anthropologist. Female," said another.

At customs, the dental impressions were indeed broken, with appealing care, to see if they were filled with gold. It occurred to no one that the plaster might be a disguise for heroin or cocaine. As no gold spilled out, the customs men concentrated on glueing the impressions together again and gave them back to her labelled "No gold."

"In the West," Wanda said, putting her rings back on, "there is an advertisement for diamond rings that says 'A diamond is forever.' Except that they've changed it to 'A diamond is for now,' because people want things that are now, now." Seeing no way out of this sentence, she rushed into incoherent chatter about the crash. The chatter was reported to some authority, and she sat alone on a packing case for several more hours before she was released. Only in Poland, she thought.

And only in Poland, thought Boleslaw, speaking German in Gdansk to the younger strikers, because he wished to seem a good marketing Pole of the new order. But he found an old shipyard employee who had been in the yard in the French-speaking long-ago, when his own sailboat had needed an overhaul on a voyage that he was undertaking on a route once sailed by Shackleton. The old worker nodded at Boleslaw's picking him out to speak to in French. "German is necessary as the language of the economic miracle that is missing us, and Russian is not to be preferred," he said, also in French. He tied a bowline around a bollard, his tough hands at odds with the lean cut of his thought. He added, with a very Gallic flutter of his calloused hands, "French is the language of diplomacy, and Poles have never been diplomatic with Russians. We have been used as a corridor too often."

Boleslaw said, "And shrunken too often."

The worker went on, coiling another line, "There is a medal of St. Stanislaw, engraved in our alphabet and not in the Cyrillic, that was awarded by the Russians to heads of the militia who had significantly overrun our country. When the Czarists hit hard times, they sold their jewellery, and there are many of these medals in Poland. We have appropriated them, because they are beautiful in design, however ugly in meaning. The Writers' Union Awards, too; undeniably fine. Czarist pendants given to foreign members to whom we cannot pay the deserved zlotys. You will please not say that I can speak German.''

Only in Poland, thought Boleslaw again, who had been honoured fearlessly in Polish a year before by the Journalists' Union.

Back in Warsaw, a while later, Boleslaw was on the loose in an English library endowed just before the war by a rich Englishwoman widely loved and widely regarded as batty. The place was staffed by Polish-loving English remnants, mostly women, some quite young. He had his own second-hand and unused copy of *Divas of Yesteryear* to fall back on—never go into a house of plenty without provisions of your own—when he felt himself to have bumped into someone.

Wanda. It was actually Wanda who had done the bumping. But Boleslaw, a skinny man, saw others rather as he would see small and rocky Sheraton tables: probably reproduction and badly made, definitely cause for spilling. So he lifted his book, in lieu of a hat, and apologised.

"Again you don't remember me," said Wanda.

"Yes, I don't," said Boleslaw. Though he did indeed, of course, even if not yet her name. He went over what he had said, and found the haplessness impermissible. Wanda left the library carrying a pile of notebooks. Boleslaw noticed that she had a list on top of them. He remembered that someone had once said that making lists was the mark of a poet. He went up to a librarian and asked if she knew who had said it. "Or writ-ten it," he added. Other librarians joined in the hunt, but it was near closing time and they retreated to guessing as they were putting books back into the stacks.

"Does it matter?" one said.

"Well, it's better to get things right, isn't it? I got an au-thor wrong just now," said an official with eyebrows that he would lift in apology as others lift their spectacles.

"You could try Auden," said an elderly librarian. "If only he were here to ask," she added to herself. "I think I never saw such a fine face, apart from Mr. Beckett's."

A partridge-shaped librarian with a very tight and nurse-like belt whisked Boleslaw from library thought to reporter's fatigue in a moment. She whispered unsympathetically that the dictionaries of quotations were in the reference section and the reference section was closed.

"I'm not making for dictionaries, I'm making for Auden," he said. Frowning in rage, he turned back and asked her if she had a volume of the latest book by the author of the one under his arm.

"Author?"

"Flora Stuberdale. *Divas of Yesteryear.* A key work of its time." He stabbed his finger at the list of her other works on the flyleaf. "It's her next one I want, you see. *Lesser-Known Divas of Yesteryear.* You won't have heard of her."

The librarian took the insult in her stride, as she always did near closing time, and said, "She'd have got a flipping Foyles' Literary Lunch for that, I bet," and looked up the title in *Books Out of Print.* "O.P.," she said. "Out of print through demand, I expect."

"Do you happen to know the name of that young woman in the trouser suit? The one I bumped into? I used to know her. Ages ago."

An even harsher librarian took over and said, "We can help you with the names of books, sir, but the names of library users are not part of the service."

"Some people are doomed to sound farcical," Boleslaw said in the low murmur he used when talking to himself, "but I'm sure you don't mean to sound like a record."

"The record department is shut," said the librarian.

"This day is a granny knot," said Boleslaw to himself, "so it will come apart if pulled."

He read Auden as he walked back to his hotel. In the way of things, he remembered more and more about Wanda as he read. A small child when he had leaped over the electrified wire with her. The empty seat on the plane: Wanda's younger brother, killed when they made the jump. Given a little hush, many mislaid thoughts can occur at once. It is only in the noisiest conditions that one can truthfully give a single answer to "A penny for your thoughts."

Having many Polish friends in London, Wanda knew that there were three exchange rates for the zloty: the official rate, the official black-market rate, and the unofficial black-market rate. The descriptions were solemn and accurate. The official rate greatly favoured the zloty; the unofficial black-market rate, rich in zlotys beyond the dreams of avarice and a worry to anyone Polish-born, meant standing on a street corner for five minutes of dangerous observation, so hard pressed for foreign currency was the country. Wanda bought a few zlotys at the official rate and then a lot more at the unofficial black-market rate.

The concierge at her hotel, a cheap one at the centre of rebuilt Warsaw, remembered her as a little girl. He had been greatly fond of her parents, both killed in the Warsaw Uprising. She walked in the twilight past the Cathedral of St. Jan and went to a café to have some dinner: potatoes; delicious cauliflower rolled in butter and chopped hard-boiled egg; no meat. People ate together, in the Polish way, at tables for ten or sixteen, and cleared their own plates. Talk was surprisingly unguarded.

So, indeed, was everything in Warsaw. By the time she had strolled back to her hotel, she found Boleslaw there, by a wonder. Without a beard, though he had been very much bearded on the plane. How had he found her? By chance? No. He was, after all, an investigative reporter. No miracle, just slog. They spoke Polish, eschewing the German they hated. After her brother's death, left unspoken of, they had made it separately to England with the sometimes magicked heels of the young, and there never found each other.

"I lost heart that I'd ever see you again," she said. "But then I found you on the plane."

"Vital things can take a long time," he said. "It's only gradually dawned on me."

"But it wasn't that long ago. We weren't that young."

"Pre-student."

"One's always pre-student. And also always retired, of course. Cart horses put out to grass." At that, Wanda saw something equine in the face of a hotel resident passing by, a man who had lent his bedroom key to her when she lost hers and they had together discovered that one key worked for every door except the linen cupboard, the babushka's terrain. Wanda waved. The hotel guest, who had made no passes at her, merely bowed his head gently.

"Is that a boyfriend of yours?" said Boleslaw, twisting a coat button.

"No. But debonair."

"I've been waiting for this to happen for a long time," said Boleslaw.

"The man?"

"No. Finding you again."

"You couldn't say it was instant recognition."

"No, but you could say it was slow dawn of recognition and be just as commonplace."

"I don't see anything commonplace about you. You haven't picked up anything trite abroad."

"You make abroad sound like a germ," said Boleslaw. Thought and speech collided, minds merged, oiled a heavy hinge, and made things light again, as they always had been in the not forgotten days when they had leaped the fence.

14

Longing for news of him, this man in her presence, news as on a postcard, she said, "What have you been doing?"

"I worked for a while on newspapers, after a time in France. And acquired a red beard."

"Always a hot disguise. You haven't got it now." Thus the slow mulling of an intimacy dreamed lost, she thought.

"May we have an ashtray?" she said to the waitress, who was wriggling into jeans behind the bar.

"The bar is closed."

"An ashtray with water in it."

"Vodka is closed."

"Water is what I said."

The waitress obliged. Wanda, moved to sound wifely, said, "For his contact lenses." Boleslaw took the lenses out. They were coloured blue.

"Does that make you feel sick?" asked Wanda.

"Not seriously," he said.

"Your eyes are like Jesus'," she said.

"Oh Christ," he said. "No. More like yours. Much more like yours." He had a sip from the ashtray and said, for relative calm, "Yours were always brown. You were wearing brown eyeshadow when we jumped over the wire, and it smudged, but it only looked like tiredness." He wiped tears of some sort away from his own eyes and, trying gaiety, said, "These contact lenses. I have seven pairs at the ready."

She said, "A foreign correspondent has to be free to be anyone." She could hear him think "No, no one," and muttered something too soft for him to hear, in this shared learned English. Learned far away from each other, and for different purposes, except that theirs now seemed the same. To look at the tiny blue lenses afloat in a blue-and-white saucer; now they could have belonged to either of them, long lost as both were from their homeland, and primed at any moment to take on disguises.

Pause. "What do you actually do?" Wanda said.

"Watch wars and queue for the telex."

"Have you been back to Poland much?"

"Every year."

"Doing what?"

"As I said, making films and running a marionette theatre."

"Underground cabaret?" She had been imagining a tiny political puppet theatre officially unknown.

"No." For the benefit of the possibly planted concierge. "A great attendance. Many interesting bureaucrats from the Ministry of Culture."

He lit a long brown cigarette, and talked out of the side of his mouth, so that only she could hear. "Most of the double meanings slip by the censors safely. The detected ones have so far never failed to benefit from the rule preventing any Pole from coming to trial. To public trial. I once got away with a film called *The Pleasure of Your Company Is Requested at the Ribbon-Cutting to Celebrate the Train Line to Auschwitz.* I think it was the courtesy of the title that got it through."

They ran the gauntlet of the watchful babushka knitting at the end of the hotel corridor. She warned them that the room was for the lady only, and then paused, implying another warning. It was, of course, that the room had been searched. Wanda had brought with her in her luggage a photocopy of a score with three of the many pages out of order. In the short time since she had left her room, the score's pages had been arranged in the right order. It was what she and Boleslaw were accustomed to. No fault of the babushka, who was Polish down to her flat black boot heels, which looked as if they had been growing out of the floor forever. When did she sleep? Where? In her chair, between comings and goings, though never wavering in patience. Some might have called her a purchased old soul, but not anyone who knew her. She was to be trusted in her connivances, which were as much on the side of the hotel guests as her knitting was. The knitting only seemed endless because she gave the thickest of what she knitted to the thin and chilly Poles in the little hotel, keeping two pieces of work going at once in case of enemy observance.

As Wanda and Boleslaw were about to go to bed, for the first time in their many thoughts of it, the babushka knocked at Wanda's door, poked in a crossed pair of needles, made a shake of the head over them, and disappeared. Boleslaw leaped out of the door and said, "See you tomorrow, before noon, at the Grand Hotel, and ask for the plastic convention." He also disappeared. Cloaked though they might have seemed to electronic listeners, such code-sounding words were the means of surviving an infancy in the sewers of Nazi-occupied Warsaw, of electric fences bounded over.

* * *

The next day, on the way to meet Boleslaw at his more expensive hotel, Wanda found that it was one of the single
Sundays in four that counted as a day off. Carnival reigned.
Vodka was drunk, at great expense, behind charabancs. She
remembered that in Poland a potato meal is enlivened by the
saying that a potato in Poland grows dreaming of the vodka
it is going to be made into. Because of the state of the economy, vodka was extremely expensive for Poles to buy, for it
provided crucial export trade. Nevertheless, a potato grow-
er is going to be a vodka drinker, Moscow economists in
power or not. So there was a certain amount of sickness
going on behind the charabancs, though a more joyful sickness she had never witnessed. Anxious wives and children
watched with pride out of the backs of the charabancs at the
hardy prowess, and provided clear spring water and singing
as palliatives once the heroic trial by ordeal was over. There
was no clapping. Applause is dangerous, when apt, in
Poland.

In the hotel, thinking in Polish and waiting for Boleslaw,
Wanda heard Geordie English at the bar.

"Blimey," she said.

The men asked her over at once. Five of them. About
twenty-two years old, not more. They had been laid off in
England and had seen on a bulletin board an advertisement
for workers for six months in a plastic factory three hours
away from Warsaw. And payment at the official rate of exchange, with a weekend free in an expensive hotel. Knowing few Poles but knowing one another, having no idea

where life would lead them next but seeing no work for themselves in Tory England, they came.

They gave her a drink, two, and refused to let her pay. They called zlotys "zlots," said they had loads of them and couldn't take them out of the country.

"You've learned Polish a bit?" she asked.

"Not much point when we might be in Algeria next."

"You miss England?"

"What they call unrealistic, isn't it? We'd be on the dole back home," and then, breaking into song, " 'And we'll not go down the mines, Dad.' "

They were clearly cheered by the company of an English-speaking woman.

"What about the girlfriends you've got here? Leaving them behind?" said Wanda.

"Well," said a Geordie called Alan, "not much point in a lasting relationship, is there?"

Another of them carried on for him. "Not with someone you can't speak to, and they haven't got time to learn English. Not that they're prostitutes. Very hospitable. Very hospitable parents, if they've got them left."

The Geordies sang a short song, "Nice girls the zlot girls, well wortha lot girls," and raised the glasses of beer that the hotel provided free.

Boleslaw turned up and kissed Wanda, both of them remembering their code assignation with an affection not usually aroused by plastic. One of the workers, all of them sensing a need, slipped Boleslaw the key to his own posh room and said, "See you in a quarter of an hour. Telephone takes a long time to get through."

The time alone so long delayed was interrupted by a bed-maker, but bed itself worked beautifully, in the mystical way of such things in impossible circumstances, perhaps aided by the good will felt by the boys downstairs, who had no language in common with their temporary girlfriends and no idea where to go next.

"I think I should go back to England," said Wanda.

"I think I should stay here," said Boleslaw.

"I see that."

Kindred as they always had been, they left each other without ado. A great deal had happened in their lives, a great deal more would come. Anything of the present had the nature of a hallucination. Wanda shook hands with the babushka in this corridor. The babushka showed her what she was knitting. A balaclava helmet. "For Gdansk."

Even under the boot heel, people in Warsaw do not guard their words.

Next morning, the news must have spread that Wanda was back in Warsaw. An old friend named Kakia, a survivor of Auschwitz, sped on crutches into the hotel lounge, where Wanda was reading the papers. Kakia carried a bunch of freesias, the flowers of the Polish spring, which she had dis-covered she could freeze in her refrigerator to last the year round if she buried them in an ice-cube tray of water. Wanda had no idea that Kakia was still alive. She was not in the directory, but then no wise Polish Jew is: anti-Semitism still comes and goes in Poland.

Kakia was well into her eighties now. A scholarly, blithe, gentle woman. They spoke rapidly of many things. Kakia had lost her job as the editor of a film magazine, but friends helped her to manage. She could translate for them, and read possible scripts; even—not so curiously—give advice about how to deal with the Soviet-trained inhabitants of the white wedding cake of a building that dominates what remains of Warsaw.

Kakia asked Wanda back to her apartment for tea. She lived at the top of a poor block of flats, walking up there on her crutches, both legs having been broken in Auschwitz. She made tea as they talked, interrupted constantly by the telephone, for everyone trusted in Warsaw knew her number by heart. Before Auschwitz, she had found time to leave her beautiful sixteenth- and seventeenth-century family books in the care of a less endangered writer friend. She also left him the family chandelier. When she survived and came back to Warsaw, her friend had saved the belongings of the razed family house. So now, in the minute flat, the walls were packed with the volumes of vellum, and at one side of the room the chandelier hung low over the sofa, where Kakia read with her legs up beside the telephone. Somehow, in foodless Warsaw, she had found a rich chocolate cake for tea. In the kitchen, she said that she couldn't remember whether Wanda liked milk and sugar in her tea: this after such decades. "Neither," said Wanda, putting an end to Kakia's effort to open with a crutch a high cupboard.

Kakia said, "How I hate people who say, 'Just a little,' as though that weren't just as much trouble as a lot."

While Wanda was there, Boleslaw rang Kakia about a possible job for her at the Lodz film school. Kakia said that she couldn't leave her telephone or her books.

Boleslaw came round early the next day. Wanda, concerned, had already dropped in again. "Sleepless from all-night shooting and all-day marionettes and the Warsaw telephone," he grumbled cheerfully. Then he said that there was a lighter job going in Warsaw as an interpreter at the Ministry of Culture. From Polish into Russian.

"Bravo and yes. Right into the heart of the enemy," Kakia said. "Well, I've been there before and got away with it. I look older than the records and I dye my hair."

Her hair was like a sink brush; even dyed pure white it still looked like a sink brush; but the bureaucrats of the Ministry noticed nothing but her cloak, dyed red, and her canes, purposefully exchanged for her crutches. Friends helped her down the stairs. Boleslaw weighed in as usual.

Later, over a cauliflower dinner, Boleslaw explained to Wanda that Kakia had often braved it to the underground university to teach. It was now far better than the overt university, he said. Sometimes it was called the flying university.

"Why?" said Wanda, in an undertone, because Boleslaw had his red beard on and his blue contact lenses in.

"Because there's no place for it. It doesn't ground anywhere."

"But people know where to go?"

"Of course."

"No prospectuses?"

"You can't copy-print more than nineteen of anything."

"Not twenty wedding invitations?"

"One aunt too many. Always a peril. As to the flying university, it flies underground."

"Might I?"

"Seven o'clock. Lecture on Swift. The basement of the Ministry of Culture."

Every evening for ten or more, Wanda went with Kakia to the university, once to a showing of a brand-new film by Boleslaw. Kakia had seen it already, at the censors' showing, and had laughed so much that she forgot to translate for several moments and lost the job from the furious censors, who made unpleasant threats. Expulsion. But worse had happened to her: Auschwitz, the Uprising, Lublin.

Wanda thought about the film. About the injuries caused in its making and screening, taken without qualm. She decided to stay, in spite of her noticed link with Kakia, if she could find a job. She and Kakia had lunch at the Writers' Union. Boleslaw was at another table, near them. Potatoes, leeks, gravy. Wanda could not understand why talk stiffened when their table was joined by an inoffensive-looking couple, who asked her how best to translate a line from *King Lear*. She was friendly; both Kakia and Boleslaw said nothing. The couple quickly left.

"Why didn't you speak to them?" Wanda said in a low voice.

"Party hacks," said Boleslaw cordially, eating up the left-over potatoes on the couple's plates, which they had failed to clear away. Wanda left quietly, not looking back. Boles-law stayed, observer that he was.

THE NUISANCE

A WOMAN ON HER OWN, in a knitted hat and navy-blue mackintosh. Thin, no makeup, kind face, wrinkles around pleasant eyes. She stands at a table in a bacon-and-chip shop, apparently waiting for something. She looks at the open door.

"Cold, isn't it?" She speaks to anyone.

A fat woman with her back to the door says: "I don't feel it."

"It's cold, I said. Isn't it?" Pleading.

"I don't feel it."

"You're all right, then?"

"Close it if you like but I don't feel it. I don't mind what you do."

A young girl sitting at a table with her boyfriend shrugs, gets up, closes the door herself.

The thin woman hasn't anything else to talk about for the moment. She sits down with a cup of tea, undoes her shoulder bag, which is pinned together with a safety pin, and puts the pin in her coat like a nappy pin. In the bag there is visible a folded evening paper, a handkerchief, and something wrapped up in a grocer's bag that has been creased and flattened out and reused several times so that it is soft and pliant, like a fabric. She takes out the paper bag, unfolds it, and sets half a buttered roll in front of her on top of the bag. The man behind the counter looks at her, because she hasn't bought anything, but trade is slack at three-thirty in the afternoon and there are empty tables, so he says nothing.

"Makes you sick, doesn't it?" she says, in a loud voice. Her tone is conversational, as though she were passing down a village street full of people whom she saw every day instead of sitting alone in a Blackpool café off-season in the presence of strangers.

"This weather. You can't wait for spring, can you? You get fed up with it."

The fat woman whispers something to her friend and laughs. An old man leaves a single chip on the side of his plate in the way his mother had taught him and props a paper against the sauce bottle. The thin woman looks carefully at each table in turn and then goes up to the counter for a cup of tea.

"No sugar. I can't stand sugar in tea, can you?" The owner of the café turns the steel handle of the urn and pushes a sugar basin at her with the tea. She sits down again with her hands in her lap and looks at the cup for a time.

"What a lovely cup. I do like nice china. I can't seem to

fancy tea in a thick cup." The girl sitting with her boyfriend makes a ga-ga face to him and giggles.

"The reason I'm on my own is I enjoy it. I can't stand people who don't know how to be alone, can you? Neighbours, neighbours, neighbours, you can't hear yourself think with the sort of neighbours I've got. Talk! Sometimes I think I should go and find a desert island. How many words do you think they get through in a day? Thousands, I should think. Ten or twenty thousand. Will they leave me alone? I ask you. Their noses are longer than their arms. Chatter chatter chatter. Keeping you gossiping when you're in a hurry. Get me? I've got a lot to do. I haven't got the time."

She falls silent for five or ten minutes. The old man finishes his paper and goes out without looking at her. The young couple play a game with some matches and press their noses together. The fat woman and her friend collect their shopping bags onto their knees and then go on sitting there, muttering low enough to be able to hear her when she speaks again without having to acknowledge that they are listening. A workman in overalls comes in and collects a cup of tea, a ham sandwich and a slice of apple pie at the counter. He looks in her direction when he turns round with the plates. She moves up in her cubicle and shifts her roll and the cup to make room for him, and then watches him sit down at another table. After a moment she goes up to the counter.

"Give me a ham sandwich and a slice of apple pie, will you, love? The pie looks beautiful. Homemade, I expect. I like cooking with materials, don't you, not with a tin opener.''

The owner looks irritable and takes his time. She stands there silently for a few minutes and he tells her to go and sit down. He ignores the existing pile of ham sandwiches and makes another one, using margarine out of a packet instead of the mixture of butter and margarine ready in a white pie dish. While she is waiting at the table she opens her shoulder bag again and counts out the right money, putting it neatly into a pile of coins with six coppers at the bottom, then a shilling, then a threepenny bit, and two sixpences at the top.

"I'm lucky. I live in a corner house. I pity people in the middle of the row, don't you? Houses each side, everlasting chat chat chat over the fence, heads hanging over like horses. I've just got them on the one side. They don't wait for me to speak, you know. They break the ice straight off. When I had my baby my husband was away, and my neighbour said I only had to knock on the wall and she'd come. Mind you, she said she weren't forced to hear me, but I took that as a joke. I soon put her at her ease. We laughed—you should have heard it. I'm close, of course. I'm a Cheshire cat. She don't call me by my Christian name. I don't care. You might say I'm the square peg. When I run out of tea I don't go knocking. They come round to me all the time, they drive me mad. That's the beauty of living on your own, isn't it? You don't have to speak to anyone if you don't want to. My mum used to say to me, you shut your mouth or I'll put a sticking plaster on it. She took me out to work with her when she was in service and I'd sit on the potato urn hour after hour just watching her. Only once I got on her wick, shouting I expect like children do, and she learned me a lesson I'll always be grateful for though I didn't appreciate it at the time. She shoved me in the broom cupboard with an Elastoplast on me mouth and after that I knew how to keep out of people's hair. When I got the pains I remembered that. I check the layette, then I go out and telephone the doctor, I bank up the fire with some damp coal dust so it keeps in, then I make myself a cup of tea. I take my time. You got to try not to think about things. There's never anything wrong with me. If you think about it, it gets a hold on you. Then I wind up the clocks because I never like to see a clock run down and I don't know how long it'll be before I'm up and about again. I lie down, then I get up and make a sandwich and put it by the bed in case I fancy it but by then the pains is coming quite fast and I don't want it yet. Then I lie down again and listen to the clocks ticking and think, by the time I have that sandwich there'll be a baby in the house, making such a racket I won't be able to hear myself think; I'll regret it I shouldn't wonder. Of course I know I won't but I make myself laugh. Because I've got used to being on my own, you see. I don't depend on company. The time goes by. I thought, my time's my own, I wouldn't change places with anyone in the world. Then the doctor won't come and I start not to feel too good. Nothing to write about, though. I bang on the wall, more to take my mind off it than anything. I knew she were in because I heard her kettle whistling. She were in the room right next to me. It's only a partition wall and I could hear her moving about. She weren't deaf neither because she used to complain about the kids on the other side of her. You wouldn't think anyone would let a baby die just because it was going to cry, would you? But I'm right. I know I'm right. I've been over it in my mind. The truth is she's a single woman and she's jealous. She's never been married. She don't know how to converse with people. In the case of my husband she was jealous because he was a gentleman, like a doctor. He had a beautiful sunny disposition and he indited the best letters a wife ever had. He were away in the navy in Hong Kong etcetera and I got a letter from everywhere he went, sometimes a picture postcard and sometimes a letter airmail. When he were home in the old days he used to go fishing at the weekends and he'd sell the fish and put it towards a motor bike. He bought a B.S.A., not secondhand, it cost two hundred pounds, he used to clean it with Min cream in the evenings and I'd stand in the door so the light shone out for him and we'd talk and laugh until gone midnight and then sometimes go out for a spin with me on the pillion. I expect that was what got her. Then when he were off she started getting her knife into me because she knew I were on my own. But I can stand up for myself. I don't need her. It were just that time. I'm glad she didn't come when you think about it because she'd have made a nuisance of herself. I were better off on my own."

THE
WIND-CHILD
FACTOR

S IX PEOPLE WERE WAITING for Bertram Wood in a Chinese restaurant in London. All dons, all learned, all men. Five vying men, one hungry man.

"I wonder why he chose a Chinese restaurant. I mean, why not Greek or Italian? As he's a classicist."

"Or a bar, as he's a lawyer. Called to the bar."

"He probably speaks Chinese. That would be it. Mandarin Chinese."

"Bertram Wood a Mandarin man? Never. He's his father's son."

"There's a new translation of Proust that has the phrase 'deliquescent mandarin' in it." No one knew how to react. "The phrase itself, *mal choisi* though it may strike our dumb ears, does express the very essence of a deliquescent mandarin. Sonically."

"Perhaps that's what the translator meant." Pause. "Or Proust. Are there any nuts?"

"Was the phrase in a Bertram Wood translation?"

"He says he's not up to Proust yet."

"He's up to anything, Bertram Wood is. Did you know he plays the harpsichord, the clavichord, the piano, and the Hammond organ?"

"In the old days there used to be prawn crackers at Chinese restaurants, but now there are only crispy noodles and I don't like crispy noodles. Do you think we could get some fortune cookies in advance?"

"Bertram Wood must get hungry, too."

"He would have that from his father. They liked cooking for each other. I once saw them at it. More in the interest of cheering each other up than because of what they called being 'ravenious.' They got through poor times together."

"The hunger wouldn't be from his father. It would be from his background in the war. The Second World War."

"Good Lord, was he alive then? His whole future still seems to lie ahead of him, though he's already achieved so much. In many fields. We should get him talking about the Goncourt brothers."

"Or tennis."

"A manifold man."

"Has anyone done anything about the Chinese fortune cookies?"

"He shares a house with his stepmother, doesn't he? Joanna Something. They live just round the corner. We could ring to see that he's on his way, but if we got her we'd have to ask her, and she'd contribute nothing."

"We'll merely have to wait."

"Doomed to wait. This is our fate. Waiting for the great."

Someone sensible groaned, and stole some leftover Chinese fortune cookies from another table.

Forty-odd years ago, Bertram was already being similarly harrassed. When he was ten or so, he was asked by a red-nosed but spiritual-looking Sunday-school mistress, "And what is your thought?"

"It is in the matter of God that thought has given me most disappointment," he said.

The Sunday-school mistress held the top of her nose between her right thumb and middle finger.

"Are you going to sneeze?" said Bertram.

His best friend, Sam, kicked him, because everyone else at the Scripture class could see that she was furious. She wore an old grey cardigan that affronted the boys by its lack of fastidiousness, and grey stockings that had a red ink stain on one of them. The girls in the class bet every day on which leg would be bearing the red-ink-stained stocking, suspecting that she went to bed in her clothing.

"Have you got a cold?" said Sam. The children were not joking. Sympathy for the woman ran through the class like a wave through sand, now that her embarrassing attempts to force them to act out the Book of Ruth among the desks had been laid to rest.

"I'm holding the right thought," said the Sunday-school mistress.

"It's your nose, though," said Bertram. "Have a peppermint."

"Peppermints help colds," said Sam, a loyal trooper, pursuing his friend's foiled try at peace.

"Peppermints better *hinder* than help colds," said the Sunday-school mistress, and the children took their elbows off the tables. The class had more feeling for her when she was pedantic than when she was vague. So she tried a question. "Perhaps peppermints better hinder than help colds? That would be what you mean?"

Bertram held on to the possibility of her charity, because he had to go to the dentist the next day. The dentist was known as being "good with children," and Bertram was to have all his baby molars out. He counted them before he left the house the next morning. Eight to go. He went on his bicycle, preferring to make his own way.

"Do you like this new Teddy bear?" said the dentist, Mr. Powell. "For children younger than you, of course."

Bertram handed him an envelope with a letter inside. "My parents said I haven't got to have an anaesthetic." The letter read:

Dear Mr. Powell,
    Bertram our son does not have to have an anaesthetic. He went black under your last anaesthetic.
                    Yours affectionately,
                    Mr. Wood

The dentist said, "Why don't you like anaesthetics?"

"Ever since the last go your chair has made me think of when I was unconscious." He paused. "If a thing's there, you don't like it to remind you of when your mind was dead to the world. Beds do it too. For a thing to remind a person of being unconscious! Beds are a waste of room space."

"Do you want a throat lozenge?"

"No thank you. I like that pink warm water, though. I'd like some more."

"Not too much."

While the dentist was turned away to his instrument table, Bertram gave the Teddy bear to the nurse.

"Have you got a name for him?" she said.

"Yes."

"What is it? We'll put a label on his back."

"Exit."

"I think Felix would be nicer. Felix means happy."

"That's O.K. He's the surgery's Teddy bear, so his name's up to the surgery. Everyone grown up seems very happy, considering it's the war. Did Sunday schools and dentists stay behind as a war duty to cheer everyone up? I expect that was it."

"Only a tiny stab," said the dentist, turning round.

"No, just pull them out," said Bertram. "It's only eight of them."

"It depends what we find."

"We? It's you looking. And pulling. So pull. Please."

"Well, old boy, a few hard yanks and we're done. It's a bit like the planning of a shipyard's work. We've got to get the little frigates out of the way to make room for the big battleships."

The dentistry was done without the afterpain of an apparently broken jaw which Bertram had gone through at earlier sessions for a mere filling. Mr. Powell took the Teddy bear from the nurse's desk and propped it on the mantelpiece. "Look at him," he said. "There he is, watching us and saying what a fuss about nothing."

Bertram shook the dentist's hand. "I hope the other teeth today are more interesting," he said. "Could I have my lot, please?"

"Why?"

"I'd just quite like them. They're more mine than anybody else's."

"My regards to your mother."

"She's not back from fire duty yet. She's got you down for Tuesday."

"I should go home if I were you. Rinse with salt water, warm, to stop the bleeding."

"I'm not allowed to be there alone, because of the bombs. I'll have to go to school. Smithereens, that means another letter, saying why I'm late."

The nurse rapidly typed him a note and gave it to the dentist to sign. Bertram sighed, the heavy sigh of a child's relief. "That's one thing done."

* * *

40

After the war, Bertram went to Edinburgh University and read mathematics and English on a scholarship. His father, Bernard, visited him there once and asked, "Why can't you ever decide what you want to be?"

"I've always decided. I've always wanted to read books in as many languages as possible and to think about them. And to write things down. Though I'm more interested in mathematics. It's not a *cover*. It's perfectly possible to believe in two things. You do, in fact. Much more than two. You do masses of things at once. You still love Mama, and you love your second wife."

"Joanna."

"Yes, but you've only told me about her so far."

Bernard Wood sucked his pipe. "She's tall and gentle, and unfortunately she keeps very long hours. Last week she'd been working till two in the morning and rang me on the intercom at four from the sofa, because she didn't want to wake me, and said she couldn't go to sleep."

"She rang you because she didn't want to wake you," Bertram repeated, not as a question.

"Well, I'm sure it would have been after a very long time of hesitancy. I'd heard her walking about and boiling kettles. Boiling hot water in kettles, I should have said."

"Except that nobody else does. Nobody else, nobody else in the world, would have corrected himself about that except you. So what did you say?"

"I wanted her to come upstairs, but she thought she'd be sleepless. Her bitterness all lay against the sofa. I could see

41

no reason in it, none at all. I asked if she'd tried lying down, and she laughed and said she hadn't thought of it. So then the house grew quiet and I came down and went to sleep next to her, though there was not much room for the dog. The dog serving as a bolster, these being chaste circum-stances.''

Bernard started to cook crumpets, which he painted with the whalemeat oil that his son kept in an old paint tin. "This tin is sterilized, is it?'' he said softly, as if unassimilable other lives hostile to mankind and inhabiting tins might hear him.

"Boiled and boiled.''

"Whalemeat oil! It seems a lifetime we've had of it. Hold-ing out promise of sirloin and then letting you down into brisling at best.''

Bernard and Bertram dug into two crumpets each. Ber-nard said, "For some of us, different things take a different long time. Will you promise me something?''

"You asked me that impossible question when I was nine, and I said yes, because I thought you were going to ask me to promise not to smoke or drink before I was twenty-one, and then you made me promise not to marry a lady cellist from Budapest. Not a particular lady cellist, any lady cellist. From Budapest.''

"Well, you didn't,'' said Bernard with satisfaction, "and look how well the abstention has worked out. Oh, yes, this other promise. Will you promise me something?''

"Of course.''

"Will you promise me not to become a constitutional statesman?''

"Immediately. Why?"

"I've been thinking about it and the dangers for you in general, with your mind and the world's courting of it, and you must remember Bagehot was right."

"Walter Bagehot."

"Walter Bagehot. His prescription for a constitutional statesman was that it needed the powers of a first-rate mind united to the creed of a second-rate man. I passionately, quite passionately, believe that you would be incapable of a second-rate creed but you might think it necessary on behalf of our benighted planet."

"You once said to me, after you'd taken me out to the Proms the night I'd had all those teeth out, and you'd lent me one of those beautiful linen handkerchiefs, which I'd probably ruined for life—well, you said that the value of life lay in behaving decently in indecent circumstances. As we were at the echo part of Albert Hall, and as it was the Mozart Requiem, I obviously didn't blub, but the occasion struck me. I mean the handkerchief, the teeth, the war, the Mozart Requiem," and then he added, "fathers."

Bernard said to Bertram, lightly, "I was extremely aware of you that night."

So their minds came together, and the evening long ago, well remembered, and withstood, became prodigal.

"Whalemeat oil makes me remember chocolate mess," said the father. "You made it for me one night when you'd heard me rattling the bread bin."

"When I was cooking for you. Mamma had skedaddled."

"Not skedaddled. I'm afraid I was too much for her, or

too little. I've never known which. I miss her, don't you know. And certainly you do. Do you happen to remember the recipe?"

"It was your idea," said Bertram, loving his father's grave oddities. He had admired them all his life and, believing himself in lack, thought himself a dullard.

Bernard dipped two slices of bread into milk, and melted a mixture of whalemeat oil and butter in a frying pan ("Butter!" muttered both, separately), coated one side with unsweetened cocoa and sugar, fried the bread slices coated side down, coated the other side, turned them over, wheedled them out of the frying pan. The crusts had to be hard, but not as hard as toffee, and the rest coated with fudge but a little soft inside. The mess was perfect. The two men, both normally orderly and horrified by disarray, ate seriously with knife and fork in front of the university gas fire and found justice in their memories of triumphs over restriction.

At dawn the next morning, Bernard was asleep in the digs his son had found him, and Bertram in his rooms reading. There was a din like an incendiary bomb going off. Bertram ran in the direction of the noise of the fire engines. A house behind the Castle Mound, next door to his father's digs, had been blown up, sliced with such neatness that a staircase cantilevered from its side was still hanging in place and the wallpaper still mostly intact in the houses beside it. There were rumours of sabotage, of course—by the I.R.A., by Scottish Nationalists—but the cause was a gas explosion from the mains where someone had been digging a repair hole and had left the supply lines open overnight without a thought. The fire engines' hoses were pouring water onto flames belching out of a house to the right. To the left, the house with the clutching staircase. Where was Bernard?

After a silence, things were said fast by onlookers gathering.

"Supposing it had been the Queen," said a woman in a tweed coat over a nightdress.

"She's at Balmoral," said a landlady who knew about royalty.

"Who cares?" said a small fourteen-year-old in clogs with a slash of lipstick on her face and an Our Dumb Friends' League badge in her fake tiara.

"Don't you want to be taken home, darling?" said a lady from the North British Hotel in an ambassadorial way. "Bedtime?"

"I'm a wee whore," said the child firmly, turning her back on callowness.

A *gas* leak. Bertram, as near damnable fear as he had ever been, kept thinking of his own gas fire and the joy of chocolate mess as he hunted through the rubble. In the end he simply climbed the stairs, now swinging, and put his shoulder against the second-floor wall of the left-hand house, recently built and not of Edinburgh stone. Face covered with chalk, he burst into a room, where he found his father reciting *Alice in Wonderland* over and over again. And a woman, tall, gentle, wounded by fire in one hand, who could only be Joanna.

"You're Bertram," she said. "Your father's chest was hit by a falling timber." The room was chaotic. Rubble every-where. Surprising things remained. Looking glasses, a rick-ety mock-Sheraton table, the basin, the pretty water jar and washbowl. Bernard's spectacles were broken but in the frame only, and Joanna was holding them together in her unwounded hand as though she were herself a piece of mending tape for them.

" ' "I can't explain *myself*, I'm afraid, sir," said Alice, "because I'm not myself, you see." "I don't see," said the Caterpillar," ' " Bernard said abruptly.

"Joanna," said Bertram. "He's bad?"

"A falling beam, an architrave, did something," she said, steadying herself.

" ' "Take some more tea," the March Hare said to Alice very earnestly.' "

"What are you talking about, Father?" said Bertram, level.

"Books in danger, you see," said Bernard. "Always the first to go. We have to depend on our memories. From now on. Don't thieve Joanna from me, will you, Bertram? I realise I'd only be paying my dues—for what I did to your mother, I mean—but I'd prefer that you didn't, if possible." He lay quietly, stopping breathing, and they covered his face, and then carried him downstairs gently. He was as light as a pile of newly washed linen; in the end Joanna held him across her own two arms. It seemed well. Bertram took over in the road, and they went back to his rooms and sat awake till dawn, remembering what they could of *Alice*: Bertram not surmising why Joanna had been there all the time, both not surmising why Lewis Carroll, of all people, should be the writer Bernard chose to commit to the memory of the planet he would be buried in.

In years to come, Joanna, now mother of a grown daughter, grew even more fond of Bertram, and he of her. They saw him as the executor and custodian of his father's mind as well as of his own. More than ever alert against disorder, he added width to his knowledge of common law and became the past's investigative reporter—a self-appointed recorder of the causes of the Peninsular Wars, the Crimean War, and onward to the Jarrow Marches—and then a man of letters and a favoured pronouncer on the theatre's history. He was hard to cajole into speaking, preferring to write, though he found this stingy of himself. So sometimes he enforced putting his voice on a tape recorder, finding in this an aching link with his father's effort to imprint literature's past on some tabloid not defaceable by such a negligent catastrophe as a perilous gas leak. In the theatre, as his father had, he found lucidity in the economical, and he found warmth in Middle English's lack of clutter.

And so now overcourted. Hell's bells. He remained, always, decorous. To a woman interviewing him—Annie Jenks, a journalist honored in Grub Street for her early cynicism—he recited a bit of Chaucer and then went on to say, "And the necessities. How much is it essential to put on the stage to convey a narrative about a forest?"

"If it's a Birnam Wood on the move, that's comic what-ever you do," said Annie Jenks.

"Well," said Bertram, steady on his course, "the ques-tion—I think it was Edward Craig's originally—suddenly ex-plodes the myth that it is necessary to show a tree with all its branches and all its leaves. And in a way Brecht takes that idea and links it to an actor. In a time-honoured way ac-tors still do characters in the round, and it's very English to be so hidebound by honour." Bertram pushed on. "I can only say that the theatre, and I am a pretty rotten playwright so far, so far, is apart from other arts because of its constant re-lationship to an audience. Where else do we get the ferocity and fear that a mediaeval audience got from their religion? And where do we find the gentleness?" He jingled the house telephone for Joanna, but the house telephone was not even a house tapper and hadn't worked for many a long year.

"Where do we find the gentleness?" he said again. "On the one side, I'm the individual who thinks it's hopeless to try to change society, that we can't do anything, and that it's just like Hell anyhow. Whatever we do is just doomed to be a disaster. That's the point of Sade in the French Rev-olution. Sade is the sort of cruel visionary we find in Stalin. In the things Marat says of him."

"Who's Marat? Oh, Marat/Sade," said Annie Jenks. She waved a pen full of the ink of insight. "One person, really."

Bertram bent his head to her keenly. "That's an interest-ing idea, theatrically. And as to the actors, and the writers, more important—well, I saw something last night at a run-

48

through, and it was quite lovely for young people, but I'm worried about the substance. Though there was no contriving, and great compassion.''

"We could talk about *Finnegans Wake*," said Miss Jenks.

"In a moment. Now, this play. The life itself lightens the interior. You couldn't read it. It's not like a play. It's a piece about two young people coping with puberty, God what a word, and the girl brought something chaste to it. She had stagefright the first time. It's funny, because they're being tutored by a sex therapist, and it's all so lonely. There's a sadness. It would be there in farce. Here they're young and they don't know it. If one were able to go beyond that room the author's created, there'd be something small and gleaming. I can see it, but it would need a lot of work. Are you interested in replies? To technical problems?''

"One's got to stay focussed. I'm a born questioner.''

"How strange. I should have thought of you as a born answerer. Though you could change that, of course.''

"You'd throw in the sponge, wouldn't you?''

"Only about, I think, laundry tickets. The fear of losing them. Unclaimed shirts in Chinese laundries all over the world.''

"Would you talk about the Brontë sisters?''

"Well, everything is soluble unless it's impossible, but wouldn't it be better to talk about the theatre, because you might get more out of me?''

Annie Jenks put her feet on the arm of his sofa, taking

notes in the pad on her knees, and said bracingly, "All right."

Alarmed, he walked about the room for a time and then spoke for half an hour, mostly to himself, about Stanislavsky and Nemirovich-Danchenko (it turned out that the growingly pretty Annie Jenks had a degree in Russian), about swimming pools. "I once was in a swimming pool that had been drained and I thought this would be a way to stage Sartre, to stop him sounding like a playwright to be read from a podium, for here we have it—in the emptied pool we have our exaggerated rake, an eccentric element missing that would make thought buoyant—and if we were to put duckboard over the emptied pool and do one play on that we would have a resonance very much like the resonance of doing any play with echoes of the past by being heard through the present. You have to wreck the formality of a stage and then order it again according to the play. In the theatre you can do anything. In films, too. It's only in England and America that films are so hidebound by naturalism. Think of the wonderful scene in Wajda when Cybulski is rushing from the enemy Poles and gets caught in lines of damp laundry—sheets, pillowcases—and he can't find his way in all this waterlogged cleanness: it fills his ears as if he were underwater. It's terrifying and comic and pathetic, with all the trim hounds of Hell after him and his own bulk beating its way through housewifery. It's like having a perforated eardrum. Everything in the skull. Would you like to come out to dinner? I'm supposed to be at a Chinese restaurant in twenty minutes."

"Would that be all right?" said Annie Jenks, looking at her face in a powder compact. "We haven't got to the Brontë sisters yet."

"No, but I'm not sure I'm up to them."

"As the most famous belletrist and, of course, devotee of women's capacities, particularly when they occur in female siblings—"

Bertram had his head in a cupboard. "I was looking for an umbrella for you."

Annie said, "The forecast said there was going to be a wind-chill factor."

"In spring?"

"Well, actually I heard it from a Jamaican taxi-driver, and he said there was going to be a wind-child factor."

"Yes, much better," said Bertram from the cupboard. "I like that idea very much. Now, all these old tennis racquets. Pluck one and it's like an untuned harpsichord. Considering the damp in here, you'd think an instrument, or racquet, would find the circumstances ideal." He plucked some more tennis strings. "A very soggy arpeggio."

Annie again tried to get him to talk about the Brontës, about Sappho, about George Eliot, but nothing came of it. In the taxi she gave up.

The six dons waiting at the Chinese restaurant all had their notebooks out. Bertram went to a telephone and rang Joanna, just around the corner. Then he fell into a happy silence, ate fried rice and duck delicately flavoured with tea leaves, passed dishes, listened to the others. Most of the people seemed wary of Annie Jenks, and he acted protectively toward her. He spoke of the weather, but the table at large wanted him to talk about *Middlemarch*. He asked them about the book's own questions instead, which were not what anyone wanted.

A pall. Joanna came. Things lifted. "Is there anything you want to talk about?" she said.

Bertram said immediately, "My fingers are itching about parking at the moment."

"Secretary of the linguistic philosopher?" said a brave don, ploughing into mustard sauce for strength. "I can't quite put my finger on him. On Parking. It was a him, wasn't it? The secretary."

"No, plain parking. Parking in the street is absolutely abysmally done these days. When I walk up a road, I try every car door I can to see if I can correct things by push and pull and a little wheel-turning, but most of the manoeuvering done is beyond repair. A foot away from the curb, the front wheels desperately every which way. Two yards in front and two yards behind each car. Drivers who've obviously parked front wheels foremost. The lack of *thought*. Manually, where's the dexterity? Just a modicum. But it's so easy. Well, you long to put it right, don't you? There are streets I hardly dare to go down for the worry they would cause any decent parker."

"This is a new side of you," said an acolyte.

"Oh, no. I'm sure everyone has it. Everyone at this table. I spend a fortune on taxis or, if alone, I walk, because I happen to be quite a good parker myself and I know that if I had my very ancient Alvis under my belt, so to speak, which is no cinch to park and definitely lacking in a good turning circle, I should get distressed and try to push badly parked cars into better positions. Which would be bad for the mind. A one-up thing to do, wouldn't you say?"

"You wouldn't think he was writing three volumes about the Goncourt brothers," said someone at the table. The don sitting next to him said, "Not to speak of Balzac."

Bertram heard this and said, "You mean I'm accomplishing nothing at a single stroke." The table laughed, and grimaces denied the statement. "It's not that I'm not deeply interested in Balzac, but I'd rather try to write what I think than to speak it. A particularly curious woman whose mind interested me a good deal once said to me, 'How can I tell what I think until I hear what I say?' At first I thought it was featherbrained, then I thought there was more to it. As to parking, I can speak freely here, because I feel very strongly and have spent a good many years in contemplation of the problem. The disarray one sees in so many streets could so easily be put right by a little more attention. Or if I had the ignition keys. One simply pines to get things straight, doesn't one? This is one field that would yield to negotiation."

"The owners of the cars might be furious," said Annie Jenks.

"Oh, do you think so? No, I feel sure they'd be grateful, if they noticed at all."

"Balzac expert and pensive parker," said one of the dons, with indifference.

"No, not pensive," said Bertram with passion. "It takes very little thought, don't you see. I just have to be sure that the urge doesn't get the better of me. I could tell you some streets where the parking is well above average, and those are perfectly safe. Well, now, I'm very eager to hear what you all think of the Goncourts."

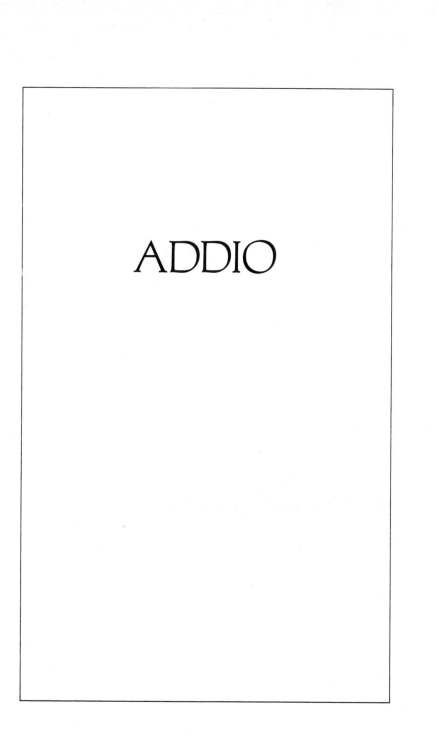

ADDIO

T HE LONDON VICTORIAN Wigmore Hall, where the
cheerful cherubs had been not even so much as
chipped by the Blitz and where the acoustics were
better than the ones bought by any number of dollars for
Avery Fisher Hall, in New York City, was less packed than
usual for the great Madame Johanna Alba's master class.
Her famed role for fifty years had been Cherubino in
Mozart's *The Marriage of Figaro*. At seventy—"too late,"
many people said—she surrendered her sprightly young-boy
part and became famous as the same opera's serene Countess. Retaining dignity, she then resisted even in her prized
master class any urge to sing her great role of old.

The two dozen semifinalists, chosen from over two hundred applicants, sat on school chairs onstage. A few musicologists were allowed into the auditorium, a few other
singers. Madame Alba was laced into her celebrated costume for Cherubino, even though she was to sing the

Countess at chosen moments. Close-fitting white waist-coat, pink breeches, pale-blue tights not supposed to bulge, though they reminded several blackhearts in the audience of the legs of a hippopotamus in pale-blue surgical stockings. The lacing of the waistcoat had been no mean feat. At last, Madame Alba, who had the musicianship to value her breath control more than her figure, commanded three holes of her waistcoat to be eased.

"We could retain the bosom," her dresser of forty years said loyally. She had travelled with Madame from opera house to opera house, like the trunk holding Madame's fa-mous pale-blue cloak for *Tosca*. Though suited neither to the role nor to the ominous plot, the forget-me-not cloak re-mained. Everyone objected. Nevertheless, Madame was to be obeyed. A resident director at Covent Garden had once contrived to put Madame into black for *Tosca*, instead of her beloved pale blue. He still bore on his forehead the scar of the marble mantelpiece of his club's main fireplace, which she had upheaved and thrown at him for vilifying her cloak at the after-opera party. Her Goliath strength was in a spirit equalled only by grand opera itself.

"Were we to retain the trimness of the bosom," said Ma-dame sternly to her dresser at the Cherubino fitting, "we should only emphasize the natural musical fullness of the waist."

So the enlarged Cherubino sat on the thronelike armchair, itself upholstered plumply in a matching pink-and-white de-sign that seemed to add further limbs to the diva's own. In-dications of plot by way of odd bits of furniture were carried in. A gold clock, a window frame empty of glass, a high-backed sofa meant not for sitting but only for the blithe fancies of rococo conspiracy. One of the few lay people in the audience of Alba fanatics, a Gregorian-chant expert named Daphne, quite unfamiliar with *The Marriage of Figaro,* asked questions of her friend Gavin, a man knowledgeable in these things. She looked respectfully at the bareness of the furnished stage, at the meagreness of the props. "It's not modern, is it? It's not minimal?"

"No. Nothing simplistic here. The impoverishment is dramatic, not optic. It is also, of course, historically lateral. The Shakespearean mockery by Mozart, for instance, in the way Cherubino is dressed as a boy."

"But Madame Alba's going to sing the Countess, it says in the programme. The students are the Cherubinos, singing bits of him one by one. And also, the Countess is dressed as a puppy-fat girl."

"This is in memory of her great days as Cherubino. A page boy."

"He must have been horribly teased at school," said Daphne, who knew more about present-day upper-class cruelty than about eighteenth-century aesthetic conventions, just as she felt more about Mozart's death in a pauper's grave than about the honour given to divas. "On the whole, I'm on the side of paupers, not of prima donnas," she said to her programme.

"Where does it say that?" said Gavin, leaning over her. "I did."

The master class began. Tape recorders were started.

Daphne whispered, "Those must be elastic tights. I wonder where she gets them." Her overriding interest was in operatic memorabilia, in the sense of clothes. Even more than in Gregorian manuscripts.

"I should think that mews shop off the Charing Cross Road would have an idea." Gavin otherwise ignored her heavily. His interest was in opera from Gluck up to, but not including, Bellini. "My passion is for *Figaro,* per se," he murmured to her severely, somehow turning the sentence into a music lover's glance backward at a hummer in the row behind. Daphne was crushed as the harpsichord began. She looked up at one of the cherubs and pondered elastic tights.

Madame Alba did not speak. This would have been a misuse of her voice. She whispered to the audience that she was going to sing the Countess an octave lower "to save my instrument." The audience rustled in passionate comprehension. The padded, page-boy Countess sang "Porgi amor" at a school desk decked out as the Countess's dressing table, looking at herself in an ornate hand mirror empty of glass. Confusion grew. The chosen students on their uncomfortable seats controlled their breathing, one or another dashing in and out of hiding and through the Countess's window at moments sprung on them by the prompter acting as stage director, and prayed that Madame would lead them somewhere in the speeded chronology fixed upon.

Again and again, the same process was gone through. Semifinalist by semifinalist.

"Where are we?" whispered Daphne.

"Round about the music master, I should say." Scant evidence of men onstage, but Gavin had confidence.

Alba's voice, distinctly hers even at an octave lower, again and again led beckoned singers to stand and to sing, in spite of the contracted plot, "Voi che sapete." Notes were taken by judges in the audience. Now and again, the director continued to order that the contestants scuttle behind the sofa or through the window (stagecraft). Madame went on singing an octave lower. Not out of prima-donna exhibitionism but out of a wish not to be drawn into contest.

The last entrant, an immensely fat girl of clear-eyed beauty, eventually got up at Madame's beckoning. Again Madame sang the Countess in her baritone whisper. Little was left of her greatness except in her phrasing.

"It would be more difficult at that pitch," whispered Gavin, making a note of no consequence on his programme.

"More difficult altogether," whispered Daphne, her mind suppressing elastic tights. "Control."

"All musicianship is control. Or, rather, liberation controlled."

"I wonder why we go to concerts together." She wished her words back, and thought them again, as though using invisible ink to rid her mind of them.

"Liberation controlled," repeated Gavin, ignoring her trouble and gripped only by his own last words, touching her spinster hand to take the chill out of his edict. He had no idea that she was blaming herself. He was not one to impute impulse.

The big girl began "Voi che sapete." Solemnity gripped

the audience. This was the voice of the evening, a voice that would never have a chance, because of the girl's size. The exquisite melody took flight. The rising cadences seemed to be drawn up by something more than the flowing of notes. No passion that music cannot raise and quell, thought Daphne in counterpoint. Dryden. Gavin looked round at her; a fidgety man, but she was not to be interrupted in her concentration.

Madame Alba rose from her judge's seat and softly joined the melody, recognising greatness. First she sang an octave lower, then in unison. A marvel was occurring. The uncast-able girl finished and went back to her seat. Madame stayed standing, without realising it. No one in the audience knew what to do. Shout bravo at the brilliant bulk? Throw roses? Where from? The harpsichordist had his head on the key-board. He had been told to keep Madame's voice down an octave, and he had failed. Then he got up and bowed to the girl's success, raising his hands. Madame Alba was still standing, hands clasped together like a singer's at practise, tears streaming down her face. Someone in the audience shouted, clapping, "Your career is at the BBC. Go to the BBC," and the applause broke out. Madame Alba said, "Yes, the BBC," her own bulk looking fragile as she went up to the girl and shook both of her hands.

"Very good rendering," said Gavin.

THEY SLEEP WITHOUT DREAMING

"All happy families resemble one another, each unhappy family is unhappy in its own way."

ANNA KARENINA

THE RIDLEYS OF NORTHUMBERLAND were an exceptionally *happy* family and quite unlike any other. Tolstoy's opening howler early raised screams of glee from the Ridley children, especially from the doughtiest, Arabella, and from their Norland nanny, Miss Rosa, and even from their frozen North of a governess, Miss Adda. As Arabella saw things, all the families they knew were happy and all in quite different ways. The Trevelyans were happy because of their sheep. The Fenwicks were happy because they all blew musical instruments. The Douglasses were happy because they were interested. This applied also to the Ridley children, whose parents plied them with possibilities of interest. Mr. Ridley was an astronomer, a musicologist, and an organ-tuner. Mrs. Ridley ran the North Country Women's Association, caulked sailing boats, and chose books for the local library.

The children numbered six. Arabella came at the start of

the first three and Tory two below; there was a short gap before the next three, but Mr. Ridley said, with a sigh signalling his usual hopefulness, that interims were born not to last. Non-lastingness, he said to a worried Miss Adda as he was ploughing through a small mouthful of kedgeree, is in interim's nature. He said such things whenever Miss Adda, valued, showed signs of leaving.

Miss Adda was in the library with Mr. and Mrs. Ridley. From upstairs came the sound of the family chant as the children came down its polished banisters: "As happy as the Fenwicks, as happy as the Windsors, as happy as the Ransomes, and quite unlike are we. And quite unlike are we, oh *boy,* and how unlike the old Count *Tolstoy.*" The children knew all about the Tolstoys' habit of keeping malevolent diaries about each other and leaving them around the house for the gutted but still furious spouse to read.

"It's gross," said Arabella, our heroine. She had been named after Strauss's own heroine by her father, but after that his fancy for such names had apparently dwindled to nothing more than naming a yard kitten "Naxos": the two next daughters, he said firmly to his wife, were not on any account to be Fiordiligi and Dorabella. "That would lead nowhere," he said.

His wife said, "As though it weren't you who'd started this opera thing. I wouldn't do it to a dog." Pause. "Or kitten, in the case of Naxos."

"That case is entirely another case."

"Men do have a way of making forthright declarations against what they began in the first place."

Cherubino, Alceste, and Florestan followed the first three.

"Mr. and Mrs. Ridley," said Miss Adda, "what I want to know is, when is there going to be another little one to teach French and drawing to?"

"Your French and drawing have outrun their course. Figaro is fifteen. He's not going to get into Oxford on the harp," said Mr. Ridley.

"Cherubino wants to be a burglar and that's another worry for Miss Adda," said Arabella: not one to see herself as a spokesman, but the family and Miss Adda were exceptional audiences, and she had an exceptional feeling for tutors and tutelage.

"So he needs access to the newspapers," said Mrs. Ridley.

"They spend far too much time in the servants' hall," said Miss Adda.

"Where do you go in the evenings, then?" said Mrs. Ridley.

"I hop on my bike and take calculus from the head librarian." As Arabella, under pledge of secrecy, admired. The house was not hapless in its alliances.

"There you are, you see. All prepared for the older ones, in the nick of time. Mr. Ridley will teach you Latin and Greek in a trice."

"I never did understand this place," said Mr. Ridley, calm in outrage. The whole household silently upheld the defiance of exclamation marks or explanatory dashes in the speech of this student of lucidity. "Not its doings, not even its furniture. Only warm place is the linen cupboard. In North-umberland, darling, surely it would be sensible to have long double-lined velvet curtains? What are these violet chintz things from Peter Jones?"

"Short," said Arabella. "And they let in the cold. Three cheers, I'm for Daddy. I hate violets. Niminy piminy."

"I'm not darling," said Mrs. Ridley. "Not in the least, for now."

"I don't mean old Adda was niminy," said Arabella.

"Piminy," said Miss Adda, cleaning her spectacles with a scented tissue.

"They know me there. When we're broke they still send," said Mrs. Ridley.

"But what I want to know is when there's going to be an-other baby? I've got to look after my continuity," said Miss Adda.

"That's our business. Might be any day, as we choose," said Mr. Ridley.

"Dear Miss Adda," said Mrs. Ridley.

"Ha-ha-di-ha-ha," sang the three youngest Ridleys. "More happy families no longa." Arabella was sitting hid-den under a floor-length table cloth. She was used to being seen and not heard, the nanny phrase to which she always muttered back, "but wishes to be"—certainly in truth and perhaps in self-encouragement. She lifted the off-wind side of the cloth and shook her head violently at her brothers and sisters.

"Young as they are, they'd better have some calculus," said Mrs. Ridley. "We loathe spoilt children and there's not one of all six of them who shows a sign of exertion except in this midnight prank of Arabella's. Slipping down knotted sheets from the bedroom window. What's it for?''

"She's teaching elopement to the others," said Miss Adda.

"Her main interest is not in lovers but in transportation, I think. She's aspiring to a van."

"Also to teaching and being taught, which might be a rose-strewn path to a profession somewhere. Durham, Sussex, even Cambridge. Like stooping in the race to pick up an apple. The race will still be won."

"I think you need a helper for them," said Mrs. Ridley.

"You can divide the children into half and use the dinner gong for change of classrooms and break, and Miss Rosa can get the bottom three dressed for sports."

"Or hips and haws expeditions while Miss Adda and I do classics with the top three."

"How far did you get, Miss Adda?" said Mr. Ridley.

"My brain at school really stopped about classics after a Latin pun. Something about *lucus a non lucendo*. My Latin master thought it was so hysterical it should be in a music hall act but I never saw any joke in it at all. Romans would be different, I daresay."

"Was he keen on music hall?" said Mr. Ridley. "Beats Latin into a cocked hat."

"My word, he was a stunner. Especially at falls. You shift the weight in your mind to get it into your head and away from your feet—your weight's never in your feet—by saying things in rhythm to yourself. Trochees, dactyls, spondees, as it takes your fancy. That's how he taught us Latin verse." Excited, she stood erect on Mr. Ridley's desk with her head up and her skirt tucked in and did a complicated series of falls and backbends and somersaults, very long, muttering as she went.

"What was it you were saying?" said Mr. Ridley.

"*AVE regina coelorum,*
Pia virgo tenella,
MARIA candens flos florum,
Christique clausa cella,
GRACIA que peccatorum
Dira abstulit bella
PLENA adore unguentorum,
Stirpis David puella.
DOMINUS, rex angelorum,
Te gignit, lucens stella,
TECUM manens ut nostrorum
Tolleret seva tela.
BENEDICTA mater morum,
Nostre mortis medela.
TU signatus fons ortorum,
Manna das dulciecella,
IN te lucet lux cunctorum
Qui promunt de te mella
MULIERIBUS tu chorum
Regis dulci viella.
ET vincula delictorum
Frangis nobis rebella.

BENEDICTUS futurorum
Ob nos potatus fella.
FRUCTUS dulcis quo iustorum
Clare sonat ciemella.
VENTRIS sibi parat thorum,
Nec in te fabris horum
Languescat animella."

"Meaning?" said Mrs. Ridley.

"I'm quite out of breath. You don't get much practise here. Well, I daresay it's dry Latin and therefore dry English, but it's an interesting trick. I believe they sang it in the Gregorian days. The soprano would hold the emphases and the choir would carry on with the rest.

"HAIL, *queen of heaven,*
pious, tender maiden,
MARY *the radiant flower of flowers*
and the sealed cell of Christ:
FULL OF *the fragrance of perfumes,*
daughter of David's line,
by GRACE *who undid*
the harsh strife of sin.
THE LORD IS *the King of angels,*
and bore you who are the shining star,
so that, abiding WITH YOU,
he might protect us against cruel spears.
O BLESSED *mother of goodness,*
remedy of our death: you ARE

71

the sealed font of gardens,
YOU give us sweet manna; in you
shines the light of all AMONG whom
sweetness is drawn from you.
For WOMEN you lead the dance
along the pleasant path,
AND break the rebellious chains
of our trespasses.
BLESSED to posterity
IS the gall drunk for us, and THE
sweet FRUIT by which the treasures
of the just resound. He prepares
himself the chamber OF YOUR WOMB;
lest our souls
should languish
for He who has made us."

"Very ingenious," said Mr. Ridley, showing the emphasised words to his wife.

"Best use I've ever seen Latin put to, as timing for acrobatics. The perfect metronome. Have the children seen you do it?"

"I don't think it right to lead them up bypaths."

"We'll install some rib-bars in the library. There's plenty of room now that we've got rid of their sainted godmother's rose-books. And we'll look for an apprentice assistant for you and you'll ship the children off to Oxford one by one."

Arabella wept to hear "Ship the children off one by one." Miss Adda heard her crying in the bathroom, and knocked.

"Come in," said Arabella. "You told me never to lock doors when I was having nose-bleeds." Miss Adda came in and said, "Not a nose-bleed, is it. Mournfulness, familiar to all of us at times." Pause. "You know you can always ask me about anything, anything at all, whenever you want. Though that's what people say, people you love, and we all forget we're going to die so it *isn't* 'whenever.' "

A possible assistant was shown into the library to meet Miss Adda. "I'm not used to talking to mermaids," she said.

"Mermaids?" said Miss Adda mildly, hanging from the rib-bars feet upmost.

"Do you train all the children with your hair floating upside down?"

"Not handwork."

"The girls *do* do practical nursing, I assume?"

"What a good idea. But I'd have to learn it first."

"I should imagine one does with everything."

Miss Adda twisted her long and beautiful legs around her arms.

"How many of them are there? Of each?"

"Three girls and three boys."

"That's quite the wrong total. It should be seven or five or nine or else you've got no fulcrum."

"I do beg your pardon, but I don't see that." Miss Adda waved one leg in a full semi-circle, then the other, with diagrammatical perfection. "Each child in the circle occupies sixty degrees. It would muck everything up if you had to put seven into three hundred and sixty. Anyway, they're not degrees, they're people.''

"It's perfectly easy with logarithms. I suppose the eldest ones are familiar with logs?''

"Mostly the younger ones because it seems to appeal to them more than stamens and stigma and so on. And none of them likes the Bible except The Song of Solomon and St. John, a choice I personally agree with. They have all conducted judicious marriage ceremonies between each other and everyone in the house, including their parents.'' Miss Adda pulled at her long straight fair hair with cheeks ballooning like Neptune's and said, "Would you be kind enough to get the hair out of my mouth? Thank you. As I was saying, no divorces, one annullment between the non-identical twins because the house parlourmaid was having an unfortunate baby by a sacked garden-boy and the children came to the rescue in a body and are doing a good deal of housework until the baby can be, shall we say, subsumed into the family—''

"Making seven after all, as I commended—'' said the right-side-up putative governess.

"There's nothing wrong with even numbers, that's why they're called 'even,' not 'unpeculiar,' nor 'odd,' as you would have it.''

"—You have only to think of Japanese flower arrangements. Beautiful things that can be made out of *one*.''

Miss Adda started to climb up the rib-bars, hand by hand, still upside down. "Are you an only child?'' she said sympathetically.

74

"Our family numbered five, including father. Mother didn't count."

"Couldn't add up?"

"No, she counted all right. Didn't count because she was a sissy. She gave me a sewing machine and nursing kit when I was two and that started the rot."

"It would explain your keenness on practical nursing."

"What is the parental opinion of sexual egalitarianism among the children?"

"As there are three of each of them, gender doesn't enter into it. The second boy stitches a fine hem. The best technician is Arabella. You'll have noticed her. She generally has a tool kit on her shoulders and rather oily fingers, though she always washes with turps before geometry or calculus or anything of the sort. She's not interested in drawing except family trees."

"Genealogy."

"No, the trees in the park."

"I regret to say that I must give in my notice."

"But you haven't arrived, notionally."

Miss Adda alighted gently on the floor of the library.

"Excuse my bare feet. It's the only practical way. Mrs. Ridley must be somewhere about. Ah, but Arabella will deal." A very old Morris had been driven up on the pathway outside the library. "Everything seems to be happening in the wrong order. You're giving your notice before you've done a hand's turn. I don't even know your name."

"Hepzibah Dunning. Isn't it awful."

"The Dunning part is nice. Arabella darling," Miss Adda

said to the beautiful, oil-stained girl who was coming in through the French windows. Arabella wiped her hands on a turps rag and said, "How do you do? I shouldn't shake hands, I stink of turps. The big end went. Don't be worried, dear Adda, it's O.K. now. Would you introduce us?"

"This is Hepzibah Dunning. She wants to give notice and your mother's not here for her to give it to because she's out distributing leaflets."

"Notice. I *am* sorry. But you've only just come. Didn't you like your bedroom?"

"I find this house very lax. This household. I haven't seen any bedrooms."

"Perhaps we should get Daddy. Is Miss Dunning here because of another baby?"

"Your father's mowing the park around the oak tree and he took some sandwiches with him because it's a long job. Arabella, the six of you would be the first to know if there were going to be another baby."

"Well, Mummy will be very sorry you're leaving and I'm sorry too. I know quite a lot of people who find the place fierce but it isn't really, not at all." Tory, a child two distant from Arabella, ran in and Arabella said, "Make Miss Dunning some lunch on a tray and show her the puppet theatre and then I'll drive her to the station and before you start asking questions be a lamb and hold your hush." She started to shake hands with Miss Dunning, then remembered the motor-oil, and saluted instead.

She dreamt nightly of being an able-seaman, of rigging, of surviving piracy and living on ships' biscuits and, most often

of all, of loading her family from a shipwrecked destroyer
into a dinghy that would hold only eight.

Later, but not much, Arabella was one of the very few
women at Oxford to read engineering. The marking was
hard on women. But like most people educated by govern-
esses and, later, by tutors, she was a long way ahead of the
rest. One of the many things she found startling about Oxford was that, though it was at the point of near-wreckage
by the huge car factories on the outskirts, every undergraduate went about by bike. How unlike all the films about college life in America, where everyone seemed to have a car
that was used as a spare drawing room. No, youth barn. She
had bought herself a gallant secondhand three-speed bike
with an enormous saddle-bag for books. A front basket
would have smelt of handcrafts, never her favourite subject.
As she sat in the Randolph one day waiting for her tutor to
take her to see *Titus* in the gardens of Merton, she made
lists. Lists had always been of solace. Lists of spare parts, of
the planets and their mileage from Earth, of brothers and sisters in age order on graph paper with twelve squares to the
inch ("The secret to life," a first cousin with close affinity to
her had once said to her, long before the metric system's
introduction in England, "is graph paper with twelve
squares to the inch"), of essential people and provisions in
any crisis, of palindromes to be lengthened each way when
time ran lightly. In the Randolph lounge she made two lists
of things on her mind.

INSOLUBLE	SOLUBLE
Get over Nelson's life and death.	*Find out whether it was Auden who said that people who make lists are poets.*
Money.	
Strikes.	
	Forget about wanting to be in the W.R.N.S.
Job.	
Go to China (£.s.d.).	*Mend sextant.*
a) Lonely ∴ three funerals in one year ∴ find new friends. But no. So.	*Learn Russian.*
	Buy drill bits.
b) Stop dreaming about Papa.	
c) Stop dreaming about Nelson and lawnmowers.	*Strip and paint bike.*
	New digs.
	Go to Lago di Orta.
	Write Ph.D. before B.A.

Her tutor was a tall man with the stoop of a giant ape, so much so that he could sometimes surprise you by behaving just like a human. Next morning, he leant out of his ivy-curtained window and yelled, "*Titus* any good?"

"I had to leave," she shouted, parking her bike. "I didn't know about the children in the pie. Our Will didn't really write that, did he?"

"Well, considering the drowning of Clarence in malm-sey and Lady M's general attitude . . . But it's nothing on *Tamburlaine*."

In his rooms—his name was Michael Young—he said, "You didn't have anything to eat before the pie scene, did you?"

"No, luckily." She had been adding "Learn to like Shake-speare" to her soluble list as she came up the stairs.

"Could you force down a crumpet?"

They had some fortifying sherry instead.

When she had written her Ph.D., in advance to save time, and then got her B.A., she came down and looked for a job. She got one on the London Gas Board as a coffee-girl. A boyfriend took her to see *A Midsummer Night's Dream* for the first time and she was enthralled by the wire-work. To hell with all my little ones, baked in a pie; this was Shake-speare. Peaseblossom, obviously a witless girl, got her fairy wings caught in Puck's wires but Titania came to the rescue and Bottom helpfully drowned Peaseblossom's moan, lifting his heavy head like a carthorse put out to grass and pining for the road over a gate.

Inspired by wire, among other things, Arabella duly be-came Minister of Transport. As usual, she dreamt in speech every night: sometimes of transport conferences, more often about Michael Young. He would be fifty now. But in dream-ing he was little more than her age and would always stay so. Politically it was a time of desuetude and neglect and she turned to her short nights, often spent on night-sleeper trains to Newcastle or Edinburgh, for thoughts of how to mend the present spoilage that was doing such harm to her land. The wrong men were in power. Thrusters, people who used everything for grist, men of no honour and no sense of history.

One of her train sleeps was abruptly interrupted by the dream-voice of Michael Young.

"You can hardly blame them, can you?" he said.

"Oh yes, I can and do."

"Yes, I expect you would. I'm very eager to hear what you've been thinking."

"Michael, I was watching the box, and the Minister of Education came on, and she cut down free school books and cut back on teachers and someone remarked on her cloth coat because she's known for her furs and she said she couldn't wear animals now because she's in the public domain."

"Do you know anything about aborigines?"

"Very little. Oh, there's an aboriginal saying that a man who loses his dreaming is dead."

"Where did you read that?"

"I don't recall. I was thinking today that this new generation, some of this new generation, this generation of mediocrities that we've given birth to, they're mutants because they sleep without dreaming. You dream, don't you?"

"Of course."

"What about?"

He didn't reply. People in dreams can't give answers that the dreamer doesn't know.

Next morning in Newcastle, after a meeting of the North-East Development Board, she ran into Michael Young. He looked much the same as ever and she believed she did too, in a red coat and red low-heeled slippers with a white wool muffler slung around her left shoulder.

"Hello. I don't suppose you remember me?" she said, holding out her hand.

"No, I don't," he said. Much distressed, she ran towards her car and let herself into the driving seat in a hurry.

"No. I do, of course I do," he yelled, through her driving window.

All shall be well, all manner of thing shall be well. A man who annuls his past is lost, a man who cleaves is found. She decided to remember that in committees, those drab places made not drab for her by thoughts of tutors, gas fires, and her father, lately arrived back from India. Indians' aspirations to world-wide scholarship commanded her respect. Her father had told her only last week that Mrs. Gandhi had told him that Nehru had fiddled while Rome burned.

BRODERIE
ANGLAISE

Grania Byam, aged fifteen, was in the Civil Service Stores in the Strand buying a pair of stockings. Stockings, then still in their heyday, were sold in the haberdashery-and-lingerie department. A most Civil Service-looking young man and his apparent wife nearby were sorting through piles of cut-price underclothes for children, the man putting them into order as though filing them.

"Needlessly messy anarchy," he said to no one in particular.

Grania started to talk to him, helping with the filing of tiny frilled petticoats and the Liberty vests she knew from her own childhood: Victorian hangovers that cut into children's shoulder bones much as Victorian ethics grazed the aspirations of the poor.

"Underclothes for sweet little rich girls and doomed little poor boys released from charity hospitals," she said. "Where do we put these? There's only one of them." She held up a pair of combinations. "Though of course a pair of combinations might be two. Implies two."

"How do you know about combinations?"

"I had to wear them when I had scarlet fever. And whooping cough at the same time."

"You're too young to have had scarlet fever. There are injections. It's been stamped out."

"Our doctor hadn't the character of an expulsionist. He had a research mind. He kept many a disease alive, learning it and moderating it as he went. He sent me a postcard every day. He was an exceptionally nice man. He used to swallow a sausage whole and then choke a bit to cheer me up about the whooping cough."

"Not very good doctoring, was it? How old were you?"

"Three. What do you do, apart from sorting out the Civil Service Stores?"

"I'm a merchant banker." They shook hands over the piles of underclothes.

"Could you tell me what P.A.Y.E. is, then?" she said.

"It's a tax system on the spot."

"How much of what one earns?"

He looked at her carefully. "If one isn't earning much, not much at all. Would you like to have dinner tonight?"

"Yes," she said. The woman Grania had thought to be his wife was gone into artificial-flower hat trimmings. "Where?"

"Simpson's? Do you have dinner much?"

"Not that much."

"Out?"

"No, in. Usually. The landlady lets me cook things on the kettle ring."

"What things?"

"Espresso coffee. And then you can use the kettle for hard-boiled eggs or Bovril."

"Is eight o'clock all right?" They shook hands again. "My name's Peter Shaw."

Grania, who was badly in need of a job, sped along the Strand. She turned north toward Covent Garden, then still very much the fruit-and-vegetable market it had been since 1828: architecturally eminent, for all that it was a home for parsnips. Glass pavilions dreaming of pleasure domes to house Brussels sprouts; spacious aisles of cabbage; nineteenth-century Tchaikovsky-ballet arches leading into halls sweet with the smell of spilled apples.

A lorry driver shouted, "Lost an earring, darling?" It was a time of earrings. Grania felt her ears in a panic. Both earrings safe. The trick always worked. She grinned. The man grinned. Laughter from the lorry drivers' tea stall.

Near the great St. Paul's of Inigo Jones—not Wren's cathedral—where she had often crept in to listen to choir practice and thought of the theatre people buried in the churchyard, she saw a sign in a window for a needlework caption writer and coffee-girl. Twenty-five shillings a week with P.A.Y.E. tax deductions. She told the advertising manager she was sixteen to get the work.

"You will be taken into an unfortunate tax bracket," he said comfortlessly.

"Not your fault," she said, true to her nature.

He coughed, somewhere between a cough and a roar. Quite a lionlike face but a weak jaw.

"You may begin today," he said, and stood. Not to show her to the door but to signify that he had finished with her. His name was Reginald A. E. Potter. His height was six foot five but left no impression. He was flat-footed and walked with rolling discomfort, like a policeman wheeling a bicycle up a hill in slow country pursuit of an axe murderer, although the path from his desk to his out tray (the point where people knew that they were to leave) was less mountainous than most of the uneven old office floor.

The building, crammed between a good cheap Italian café and a run-down expensive French restaurant, wore the aspect of a chapel. It was built in some form of dome-and-spire design. A ground-floor shop sold embroidery wools. It also rehabilitated sewing machines carrying the slogan "Make Do Merrily and Mend Every Sunday," and sold canvases stretched for vicarage chairs.

"Helm!" shouted an elocuted voice from above as Grania climbed the pious linoleum stairs. She had always wanted to be an able seaman, so the word held out hope.

A woman in Cuban heels clattered in a hurry down the stairs.

Grania was put to work on a magazine called *Embroidery Weekly*. The offices were chiefly a corridor. Upstairs were the editorial offices of *Your Lovely Home, The Little Years (A Magazine for Mothers), Fiction for Your Chaise Longue.* Along the embroidery corridor lay the luxurious circumstances of the pinnacle magazine of the group, *Madame: The*

Journal with the Dainty Flower-Arrangement Covers. This was in bold type, and beneath it, in smaller type, *"To Cut Out for Your Still-Room."* (Every word considered key in the titles of the wealthy group of magazines was capitalised, worrying the printer's readers in the foundry room in a faraway hardworking suburb.) But no rooms in this chapel dedicated to good taste were still. All were chaotic. Grania learned, of course, that a still-room, here most importantly hyphenated, was essentially a chill room, floored in marble, housing jars by the score of bottled damsons, bottled medlars, Seville-orange homemade marmalade, pickled walnuts. All marked with the month and the year in script on sticking plaster sold by the embroidery shop, and made to original recipes (called, in this building, "receipts"). The sticking plaster was made to look exceptionally like vellum used by novice nuns under apprenticeship to monks busy copying out the Bible.

Back in Peter's bed-sitter that evening, after dining at Simpson's, Grania asked him to spell out what P.A.Y.E. actually was.

"Pay as you earn. Tax deducted at source to sustain the old, the ill, the educable, and the excellent state of English road paving," said Peter dryly. "In your case, exploitation of chimney sweeps to keep up the living standards of the dukedoms, the monarchy, and the Church that own England and sit on the oil under their parklands or lock their Godly doors because the valuables inside are too expensive to insure."

"Oh," said Grania.

"The insurance companies usually also belong to the dukes," said Peter, who had been reading to her from a book of Mozart's letters to his father. "What a cheerful family. Writing symphonies and letters in bumpy carriages. All paupers." Peter's views were considered to be dangerously to the left by the hefty jokers working with him in the City. They held the position that the palaces of England were imperilled by millions of witless exiles from lost islands of Empire now looking to the National Health Service for free teeth and free wigs.

Grania had won a writing prize off the cuff for a political-essay contest a year before. Fair to lousy, her winner, she thought on reflection. But a fine deal handed out by fortune, a blue note in the humdrum key of being fourteen. Having now also won the prize of her ladies'-magazine job, she learned how to write about needlework. Satin stitch loomed. So did tapestry. She proofread diagrams of petit point and gros point. She counted characters for justified captions. She grasped that an "m" is three times as large in this computation as an "i. " She learned what a widow meant, and how poor it was in typographical ethics to have a widow bleeding in the gutter. The art direction of the magazine was far more interesting than the content. Whenever Grania set her Hermes to the galley width needed by the layout department—the em width—she much wished not to be writing in praise of daintiness and broderie anglaise. "Broderie anglaise edging adds daintiness to a guest towel." "A scalloped edging adds daintiness to a guest pillowcase."

* * *

Two years later, when Grania was married to Peter and working even harder, he asked if they could rise to a cook to do something about dinner. Grania knew she often underestimated his dinner. He was tall and thin, and needed Wykehamist starch three times a day. She found a Yorkshire cook-by-the-hour who seemed to her to possess stamina, but how wrong that was. The cook weighed six stone at the most and had a deep distaste for food. Her questions about the shopping and the cooking to be done amounted to one. "Something stewified or something daintified?" Stewified involved lumps of flour in grey salt-water-based gravy. Daintified involved parsley. This word "dainty" was becoming pursuant.

In Peter's spare hours from merchant banking, which he whisked through in half the time of most, he was teaching himself about the French Revolution and about film editing. Books on both were piled in the tiny flat that Grania and he shared in Shepherd Market. The paperbacks already read were vertically arranged in the bookshelves, but books about work in progress were horizontal. Salvaged loops of film celluloid hung on strings like laundry lines across his minute study.

One evening when Peter was working till midnight Grania had painted the uncared-for white-gone-buff of his room in a brownish green, the colour of old desk leather, to go with the roof moss on the little old Market shops. The shops obliterated any daylight. Sometime in the small hours after her painting sprint, still secret, Grania suddenly surfaced with the knowledge that Peter would forever see the new colour of his room as khaki. Peter had been landed at Normandy on D Day-plus-1. He had rescued his squad, man by man, from a flaming half-track, and won an M.C. and bar for this and many another act that he never spoke of in the daytime. But he talked a great deal about the war in his sleep, especially about his best friend, who had been shot in the head from behind a haystack with Peter a yard away from him. Khaki is a difficult colour to cover, and paint hard to find at three in the morning, but an artist friend was awake and a provider: by five Grania had turned the walls to a beautiful Florentine red, the colour of the marble that Italians often call bull's-blood, soaked in sun. It took two coats to put things right, and then two hours to give a sparkling third coat (Kwik-Dri, but still not quick enough) to the white wood-work and to paint his khaki filing cabinet white.

They were happy, poorly off, interested, solitary. They mixed the cheapest dry sherry with soda as fake champagne. They were known to a kindly old friend of theirs as "the in-separable hermits." One evening, when Grania was free-lancing at more steadying things after her day of whisking through the woman's work of satin-stitch embroidery, bad pop music was blaring from a radio on the driver's empty seat inside an inert but thunderous rubbish-collection van. Grania rang the local police station.

"There's a terrific noise in the Market and my husband and I can't work."

"We can't deal with noise. How would you describe the noise?"

"Pop from a radio plonked on the driver's seat of a rubbish van that's making a din and not grinding up anything."

"And how do you know this?"

"The van gate keeps opening and closing and the machine keeps grinding and nobody's there. And nothing's there, either."

"The pubs are still open. We'll need your name and address and telephone number. We'll send a constable to see you."

"To see me? It would be more important for him to hear the noise. Would it be possible for him to avoid wanting me as a witness?"

The police sergeant laughed, benevolently. "We promise to avoid you like the plague."

Bracing themselves, the two of them sometimes had a few friends in for dinner. Nobody mixed particularly well with anyone else, and Peter's City colleagues were the worst blenders of all. A portly Harrovian with a dimpled nose like a baby's elbow once inspected the flat in the middle of dinner.

"I say, old thing. I didn't know you were keen on home movies as well as movement in the money market. There I go, I made a pun." He laughed heartily and lit a cigar.

"They're loops of silent film," said Grania, but no one paid heed except Peter.

"A man with two sides," said a City eater of the same ilk.

"And both the same," said the cigar smoker, laughing again and tapping ash into his plate of chicken risotto.

"Many more than two and not the same at all," said Grania, less quietly than usual.

"Didn't Shakespeare say that women should be seen and
not heard, or something?" said the cigar smoker.

"Not remotely something like that," said Peter.

Hours later, after the intruders had gone their baying
course to the street, Peter said to Grania, "It really is much
nicer alone, isn't it?"

"Yes indeed."

"What happens to you for the rest of the week?"

"The usual, and then the printer's on Friday."

"You enjoy that."

"They take a lot of trouble."

"With the rubbish they have to print."

"They even read it. They've given me a book on typefaces. The only magazine they really can't stand is *The Little
Ones*. The head comp has two sons in the trade, young, and
the mother-love editorials get his goat."

"What does he call the thing?" said Peter, forking the cigar ash away from the risotto in case a cat should get near it.

"When pushed, *Flesh of My Flesh*."

He kissed her and said, "How repulsive."

The most alert day in any week of working for the fast-
selling needlework magazine was always the day when Grania went by train to the printer's in the suburbs to O.K. the
issue and put it to bed. The comps—compositors—taught
her typesetting. It was of as much interest to her as the or-
dering of words in a sentence. The comps took her out to

pub lunches and made it unnecessary for her to apologise for the nonsense they were printing with such care. She learned about muttons and nuts and bolts and leading. The head comp and she still exchange samples of new typefaces across quite large distances.

After such excellent days, the office was both tame and troubling. Miss Helm, the editor of *Fiction for Your Chaise Longue,* had developed a crippling stammer because she was in love with the editor-in-chief, onlie begetter of *Madame: The Journal with the Dainty Flower-Arrangement Covers,* a woman of unkind nature. Miss Helm tried to dress like her idol, tried to have the same hairdo, expensively dyed and set in a spun-sugar swept-up blond arrangement, but her wages were small. The editor-in-chief wore a couture toque balanced on the hairdo, but a fiction editor's ready-to-wear toque was not the same. The editor-in-chief had a crocodile bag and matching shoes, but the fiction editor's endeavour with fake crocodile was also not the same. The editor-in-chief wrote copy with a quill pen, because of her manicured long nails; the fiction editor typed on a typewriter much like a treadle sewing machine. But a typewriter means short fingernails. So no replica, no duplication held out hope. Daintified though the office was, Grania started to go about murmuring "Unkind."

"Helm!" the editor-in-chief would shout for the sharp-eared beloved above. Miss Helm would come running in her Cuban heels.

"If only Helm were an appropriate name. My second husband, who as you know died, *drowned,* looking for the buried treasure in the ancient hulks in Tobermory Bay, would always take the helm,'' the editor-in-chief had said once, laying down her quill pen and remembering. Miss Helm was taking shorthand, standing up.

"You should write a paragraph about buried treasure for your next 'Bouquets in the Youngest Fist' column,'' said Miss Helm.

"My flowers don't enter into deep-sea diving.''

"Or write a short story. A long short story about the bouquets to be found fathoms deep. A novella,'' said Miss Helm.

As well as being dainty, the office was stingy. After knocking off a score or two of embroidery captions to the right em width, Grania had to get coffee and Chelsea buns for the members of the staff in meetings. She brought the sustenance from the Italian café next door, which relayed disappointment that no one except Grania wanted anything except "ordinary'' coffee, ruling out the café's exemplary espresso. The people in meetings regularly forgot to pay her back their fourpence per coffee plus sixpence per Chelsea bun, so her wages were further diminished.

One day Grania opened a door when she was collecting coffee orders and found there a cupboard-sized room with no windows, a naked light bulb, and a woman of gaiety knitting very fast with her eyes on a pile of long knitting galleys. She was proofreading the knitting patterns by knitting them in the cupboard. The results of the knitting proofreader's work were sold by the company at a quarterly sale from which she gained neither garb nor penny. But she remained the most blithe person in the place: as good as the comps at the printer's.

Peter, a year or so later, looking into Grania's pale face, said, "You don't look exactly grey. Just white. Why don't you leave? With all the free-lancing you do, you're working enough for two."

"I will have left as of this evening, actually. The fact just hasn't filtered through to Reginald."

"Thin mind?"

"Doesn't read."

"If you can paint a room in a night, paint it twice"—and he smiled, no fool of love—"and manage the police station, Reginald's not up to your instep."

"He makes me feel part of the furniture. He's the bailiff."

"You exist. When the Civil Service Stores go bust, you'll exist. If I'd had it in the war, you'd exist." He had thought to prompt action by being harsh, but no. She sat on their broken sofa pretending to read, but the book was upside down and she lacked the nerve to turn it round.

"What?" he said.

"I didn't say anything, I don't think."

He went out of the room, softly, like a cat. Like a cat, he appeared again and lifted her up. "You're as light as a bottom drawer of linen."

She screamed, and then yelled, "Loaves and fishes! I write about satin stitch all day and I don't expect embroidery metaphors at bedtime."

"It wasn't tactful of me."

"*Tactful!* It was *stupid*. Don't go around hitting nails on the head. I gave in my notice a month ago."

Peter kept quiet, until he was in bed and started talking in his sleep as usual. The dead best friend behind the haystack. Saddened wife, listening.

Next day, after six o'clock, she went into Reginald's precipitous office to say goodbye to him.

"I read an article of yours in a journal that is not part of this group," he said. "On politics. A free-lancer is immediately fired, even for one such misdemeanour."

"But I've been writing that column for two years. And I fired myself a month ago."

"This group forbids the writing—even once, as in this case—by any of its employees for any publication that is a nonmember of the group. So I am forced to give you the sack." He stood on his uncertain floor. "It is a sorry moment for me. We feel strongly about loyalty. But those are the rules."

"But I've already *left* work here. I came to say goodbye." Pause. "Out of working hours." Reginald was in the snooper's habit of clocking people in and out and giving black marks in his mind, and on the salary sheet, to lunch-takers.

The floor creaked as he moved from foot to foot. "Let me put it another way. You're fired."

"But it's too late. I've already gone. It's after hours." Taking the initiative, because no one else was going to, she shook him by the hand and smiled and said, "Goodbye. No debts."

He led her to his out tray and yelped, "So abrupt."

The door was banged onto her nose. He had never trav-elled as far in seeing people out, so it was necessary for her to shout "Don't be sorrowful."

SUSPENSE
ITEM

O F THE FEARED PROFESSIONS, accountancy seemed to Emma the most unfavoured. Even to dentists there came more comfort, even to failed gamblers, even to failed managers of run-down bordellos. Accountants were trained in the ungentle. Walking around cities in America she had seen fear rampant in the streets as the income tax became due in April. Cash payments of a nature that was hostile to the intimations of literature falsely embedded in "bookkeeping" began to be asked for in February by tailors and barbers, and bookshops, rare-book searchers, and private libraries that would normally be festive in honour of books at any other time of the year. In London, Emma found the same mishap compounded, looming over her small, sage country suffering now for no traceable mistake of the people's historic judgment and paying in Ulster for the recklessness of, improbably, Cromwell.

The tax year in England varies according to the person

and the unexplained decisions of the line of accountants who, in any client's working life, may reach back to a martial column of four or five, beating similar drums at the arbitrary end of any particular twelve months. Emma's tax year, which could as well have ended on the day of her birth as on any other, ended on the last day of April. Oh to be in England, and so on and so on.

A fiscal date in England is like no other. It cannot, in truth, be called a date, because it spreads, in time, in every direction, like a blot on pimpled lodging-house wallpaper. The complications expand back, forth, and sideways to every point of the compass.

Emma's boyfriend was listed as missing in Cambodia. How shall we count the days? She was a teacher of the measured manners of Russian and mathematics in an otherwise chaotic comprehensive school. Maths was obligatory, though not the higher maths then taught to the pupils who were in the A stream of the school. Hers was a stream of eight-year-olds. Many of the same pupils were in her Russian class, reading the Cyrillic alphabet without difficulty, finding no hazards in the locative case or in the difference between the perfective and imperfective. She told them in February of her menacing tax date. It lay ahead a whole two months of apprehension in stasis.

"It's on your mind," said one pupil. "It would be, for a mathematician."

A boy said, "Alice thought you were counting the weeks till your chap came back. When you were making a chart at the end of your exercise book in break. I'd been watching

now and then and said probably no. It looked like a cashbook to me, I said.'' The boy's name was Eth. He had once
explained to Emma, ''You're the only person who hasn't
asked me why I'm called Eth, so I'll tell you. My mother
was playing whist after work and she heard someone gen-
teel curse 'Netheniel Gubbins!' about a hand she had. A
hand of cards. She says the name struck her.''

''My accountants keep telling me I should keep a cashbook and I try, but it slips my mind,'' said Emma.

Eth said, ''There wouldn't be time, to your way of thinking.''

Emma said, ''And there's no room in my book bag for it,
either.''

The cashbook provoked procrastination every year in
Emma. The Inland Revenue's demanded assessments were
based on their calculations from six years ago, when she had
inherited thirty-five hundred pounds from an otherwise
stingy godmother who had regularly sent her a welcome
card on the day of the Annunciation of the Virgin Mary and
forgot about her altogether at Christmas and her birthdays.

The head partner in Emma's accountancy firm was a man
who never answered letters and who smiled by creasing
lines around his inexpressive eyes, so that the eyelids met.
Nothing else occurred in his face. He came to her little
house, for an unnamed and considerable fee, in the effort to
get her to keep this cashbook.

''But it would be a waste of time,'' Emma said. ''The salary regular, as you know. But bus fares, paperbacks, tickets

to the flicks. The tube. Stamp machines. The receipts one doesn't have."

"But you must entertain. We could enter that under promotion and publicity." He looked around her minute study, which had a small table in one corner piled with books. "Your guests, leading to possible lecture appointments. They should be foreign, of course. For deduction purposes. I've seen your kitchen, in which I'm sure you do wonders in." His careful sentences often covered ground twice, like a blunt lawnmower. "We could write off the foreign entertaining as foreign interviewing, all to the good of Britannia's economy, if only you'd keep this cashbook."

"Can you tell me what a suspense item is?" Emma said.

"An item of unidentified sort referring to cash drawn on bank statements for revenue-estimated personal expenditure. Perfume, limousines, or other. For your appearances. Expenses of a personal nature." He laughed. "For all your many professional friends, you must eat personally."

She tried to hide an impatience that he did not at all comprehend, though he remarked on it. "I daresay you're suffering from something feminine," he said, laughing heartily without any signal of good nature in his face. "I shall send you my clerk and he will draw you, draw this cashbook for you once again, a copy of what I have already sent you each year. Which I have sent. Each year. It is to serve you. Benefit against tax, work, to your advantage, with which we can do wonders with."

"So what are suspense items?"

"You ask me every year."

"And each year you never answer. As an uncle who is a barrister says, you're not being responsive to my question."

He patted her suddenly and hard on the head, as if it were a wasp.

"A question is nothing to swat," Emma said.

"This lack of a cashbook. Each item or person under the current headings under which it or who is enterable should be entered. You in your position must certainly receive presents from your male friends, your colleagues. Gifts of cash presents, unless supported by firsthand signed evidence by the donor and identifiable on his or her bank statement. Subject to double tax, interest running, and penalties. Graft, wilful negligence, or criminal intent. It can all be managed by my firm."

"Out," she said.

He nodded down toward her bathroom, which was at the foot of some steep stairs, outside the front door, and shared. He said, "We could write off a third of that, a quarter of any stereo equipment, dishwasher, washing machine, varying according to its or their professional use to foreign prospects, a third of your manicure costs, tips to porters, a proportion of every item that can be agreed with the Inland Revenue. Or else you will not be able to meet the assessments, my dear, I warn you. We're in the warning business, and it all rests on this cashbook."

"One other thing I ask you every year," said Emma. "Why do the columns I have to approve read from right to left?"

"I shall send you my clerk. He will be cheaper for you than my services."

The clerk made an appointment out of hours. His name was Peter Brett. He was laden with ledgers. A puffy man, with a chin so pointed that it seemed to be formed for use as a quill pen for the beautiful handwriting in his ledgers.

"Don't worry," he said in an Australian voice. "These books are not all yours, not by any means. Your matters are very simple, aren't they? Now, what a pleasant place. Shall we move your worktable and clear a space to look at the schedules? Ten minutes will do it."

It did indeed. He had some sherry. He made no mention of a cashbook, so Emma did. "When I said I hadn't got time to keep one, your boss said, 'Needlessly messy anarchy.' What would a needed and orderly state of anarchy be?"

The clerk loyally kept his silence.

"He also endlessly, year after year, says 'With all due respect' when he's going to be contradictory. Unkind, I suppose I mean."

"Yes, he does that," said the clerk.

"To you, too?" said Emma.

"It's not only to women."

"Has he got many women clients?"

"Only one other and she's dead. He looks after her estate. She ran a building society. She hadn't got any children, and she wrote two carefully researched historical romances, always best-sellers, every nine months, because nine months is the length of a pregnancy."

"Supposedly," Emma said.

"Supposedly?"

"Any other woman in the world would know that a pregnancy is forty weeks, not nine months. I suppose it's to comfort the men concerned, but it doesn't." She turned off the gas fire, which was making a noise. "Your boss asked me last year to proofread a pamphlet he'd written about a life-insurance company. 'In any and all circumstances, to my husband and wife, delete if necessary,' it said, 'and any or all children, I attest I have given no gift.' That was where I stopped. It seemed no possible task for anyone to mend such language. Language being thought before it is spoken and there being no route to his start. And then there was something else that had been taken out, and I'm afraid that interested me more. One of the boys at school, one I showed the pamphlet to, found that he'd written 'I attest' twice more and taken it out with ink eradicator. I'd no idea he was keen on stationery. I'd no idea, either, that he was nervous about attesting. His hesitation wouldn't have been about the repetition of the word. It would have been the oath he was making."

"Yes." Another sherry and some nuts.

"This keenness on stationery. What are you keen on?" said Emma.

"Accountancy." He patted his weather-beaten leather bag of papers. It had his initials on it. It was the one sign of self-definition about him. His hair, she saw, was cheaply cut. Noticing most observations by others, he said, "Not my wife cutting my hair around a pudding basin; a barber on

109

the way to the office gets in at seven o'clock in the morning. Excellent. I like getting in early. Alone with the office pa- pers.''

"What brought you to accountancy?''

"At school a maths teacher told me that some answer I'd given was nice, and he knew that I knew what he meant by 'nice.' In the context.''

"Clues to a life.'' She had another sherry herself, diluted with soda water, which is the way she and many another had invented as the nearest they could afford to champagne. Peter Brett and she shared it. He leaned back in his chair.

"Accountancy, though,'' she said.

"I found my way to it by luck.''

"You come from Sydney, is it?''

"Quite near, by Australian standards. I wonder why people think that Cockney sounds—''

"What were you doing? When did you leave?''

"I was the son of a warder who later ran an Australian prison. He would take me into the cells of the lifers with him. He was against capital punishment all his life, but the regime sometimes was, sometimes wasn't. Terrible mistakes happened. Terrible because they were naturally irredeem- able. Before the night of a hanging there would be a deep si- lence. There are grades of silence, as there are grades of noise.''

She turned off the third variation of the Goldberg, with Glenn Gould just before the end of his short life again playing the work that had first made him famous, including the humming that sound mechanics had found ineradicable and musicologists inexplicable, though it turned out on this meditated second recording to be nothing less than a matter of holding himself to the underpinning of the modulations.

"I didn't mean music, or sound," said Peter. "I meant noise."

Emma closed the old wooden shutters. "Yes, but there was an ambulance in the street, and the shutters don't shut well against a siren."

"You once sent me a drawing of a cistern that was costing you a lot of money, and I've got it in my drawer. Not on my bulletin board. The chap you don't care for, the partner, he looks at that board. Snoops at it."

"Perhaps he doesn't know how much you care for accountancy."

"Perhaps he does, which would be why."

"I once saw a schoolmaster all in black creeping around a form room during break opening the boys' desks and stealing their sweets. The partner looks like that. Pointed toes. Lissom and pointed."

"The night before a hanging, there was a silence that drowned sense. Then, suddenly, one inmate would scream. Then others. All joined. Began to smash tin plates against the walls of their cells for half an hour maybe. Nothing to do with trying to stop the death. They couldn't. Not even any change of government changed it. One prisoner under a liberal regime was given the sentence of 'the term of your natural life and twenty-four hours thereafter.' I don't think I want any more champagne, but I'd like some more nuts. If you have them?"

Emma provided. "And?"

"And then I joined the Navy, tried to, but had flat feet, which I daresay is a metaphor—"

"Not."

"That's like your tax returns. Succinct. And then I came to England and married and I found myself a place in accountancy." He shifted comfortably in his chair. "In Australia I'd always dreamed of the City of London. I made maps of it. Threadneedle Street. Cheapside. Fenchurch Street. I got a timetable for the suburbs to Liverpool Street. Ah! And then I married a shorthand typist with wonderful speeds. They say shorthand's a dying art, but *she's* not. Sheila's no dying art indeed. Now, you see, the joy of the job for me lies in the filing cabinets, not a record lost, in comparing schedules year by year, faultless in your case, in tracking down a flaw in the partners' calculations and using a felt marker—yellow in my case—to underline the flaw that's been tracked down, by me. In this case, as I say, this flaw that's been the bane of my client for years. I warn him or her that the appropriate piece of paper will have been neatly removed when he or she comes to see the appropriate folder ('partners' property'), but I'll have passed on the information in cases such as yours, and information's best kept in the mind, anyway. It's fostered there, don't you agree? Not to say that it *festers,* not in your case. Every folder is a different person. Walls lined with folders. Wall-to-wall carpeting but from floor to ceiling. Nothing lost. All to hand." He leaned back again, after picking himself a handful of cashews out of the mixed nuts. "The splendour of it! Secretaries running over Waterloo Bridge at rush hour! The *Financial Times* ready on the desk! The Tokyo Stock Exchange on the telephone! The yen I have for it, forgive the joke. Sheila says I sing it in my sleep. But, oh dear, that awful office coffee. Sheila makes me a better thermos every morning, a thermos of espresso, the top tightly packed down, never leaks onto my figures. She understands my taste for figures. Isn't this agreeable? And you a mathematician, too."

"Do you want to ring your wife?"

"I had it in mind, but I notice you never put in for telephone bills. You should, you know. We could do something with that."

"Shall I speak to her?" said Emma.

Emma dialled his home number and said that she'd been meaning to let Peter go earlier and that she was sorry, that they'd become engrossed.

Sheila's peaceful voice from Surbiton said, "Tell him I've overkept his bacon and eggs, but it doesn't matter."

"If I were to give him bacon and eggs, perhaps?"

"He doesn't get very hungry," said Sheila, "but I know he's got a client after you, so it would be very kind of you. Not too glassy about the whites of the eggs. He says that they sometimes remind him of tadpoles."

Emma and the black-suited clerk had bacon and eggs among the books. "I'm thinking of starting my own company," he said. "I don't believe in this business of needing capital to flight off on your own. I'm going to see a stamp collector with a very interesting tax problem, very tricky. He's in a most interesting position. I believe there's a lot to be done for him with a little imaginative thinking. Many a muddle we can get the Inland Revenue out of. They haven't the time. I wouldn't exactly say they're after victims. Scant purpose in victory, but they quite relish defeat in tax evaders, and I don't fancy the thought of it for my clients. The ones I think of as my special clients. Leading the way. Up to me to smooth the path. Who knows, this chap will be Gibbons the Stamp Collector next, and you'll be Pythagoras, the first woman Pythagoras."

He clambered down the steep, narrow flight of stairs to the front door still talking to her, his heavy leather case in his left hand and she, being lighter, tucked respectfully under his right arm, as though she were another bag of ledgers. "You want to watch those stiletto heels," he said, "though I noticed you took them off under the table. I liked that." He grappled capably with the double lock and waved. "You've got your keys? Put them round your neck on a strong leather strap, living on your own." He hovered, thanked her for the whites of the eggs, and said at the door, "Well, now I'm on my way. Don't worry about the cashbook. My bet is on the client. Don't forget to declare any bribes or gambling wins. That's just something I have to say, you know. It's a ritual warning. I'm allowed to wish you good fortune." He walked off, missing something under his right arm that he thought he'd left behind.

CLIFF-DWELLERS

On board ship, on the boat deck. A young man of about 28 and a young woman of about 25, called HENRY and EMMA, are lying on deck chairs looking at the sea. A deck steward comes round with mugs of bouillon. They both take one. The sun is shining. HENRY is wearing a sports shirt and jeans. EMMA is wearing pearls and a tiara and a long dress as of Ascot in the 'thirties. A dashing, debonair young couple, at odds with the ages they reveal. Though actually old, they are not made up as old people and their movements are old only in front of the steward, their child and grandchildren.

EMMA: (To STEWARD) Oh, good.

STEWARD passes out of sight. HENRY toasts EMMA in bouillon.

HENRY: Your eightieth birthday.

EMMA: You said that last year. I'm eighty-one, darling.

HENRY: I hate being forgetful. Eighty-one?

EMMA: You're not being forgetful, you're being nice. (*Pause.*) We're both getting on.

HENRY: I don't feel it.

EMMA: One doesn't.

HENRY: I feel eager for you.

EMMA: One does.

HENRY: Thank you for wearing that dress.

EMMA: On my birthday, you've always been allowed to choose what I wear.

HENRY: And vice versa.

EMMA: Anything but jeans, in your case.

HENRY: Jeans are comfortable.

EMMA: But a uniform. You'd never be guilty of a uniform.

HENRY: That's my favourite dress. We had it made for you, didn't we?

EMMA: You did. It was a surprise. For Ascot in 1925. We couldn't afford it but you saved up on lunches. I remember noticing that you'd got very thin.

HENRY comes over to her chair and holds her by the ribs, unbuttoning some buttons on the front of the dress.

HENRY: Don't get any thinner, ever.

EMMA: No, I promise.

HENRY's face is close to hers.

HENRY: And don't get any older.

EMMA: (*Pause. She leans back her head as he puts his hand on the chiffon of her dress.*) We'll always *feel* young, even if we do get old. One does. Just as someone of ten knows exactly what it's like to be eighty-one.

HENRY: I still think it's eighty. (*Pause.*) Though what does it matter? Shall we go for a swim?

EMMA: On the top deck? Why not?

HENRY: That's one of the things I like about you. The way you say 'why not'.

EMMA: You always did like that.

HENRY: Will you marry me, Emma?

EMMA: Why not? (*Gaiety.*) But I *did* marry you. Have you got your swimming things on under your jeans? I didn't put my bikini on underneath this because the bra's bulgy.

HENRY: The bikini I like?

EMMA: Of course.

HENRY: One-pieces are senile.

EMMA: We *are* senile, as other people would judge it.

119

HENRY: Don't.

EMMA: Cheer up. It's a birthday.

She gets up. She uses a silver-headed cane that is beside her deckchair.

HENRY: Your elbows are getting thin. (*Shouts.*) You're not allowed to get thin without asking me, darling.

EMMA: There is such a thing as Women's Lib.

HENRY: We can forget about that between us, can't we? It's all over and done with. Being chained to railings. The flapper vote.

EMMA has got to her feet, fast, but suddenly wincing.

HENRY: What was that? Not arthritis? (*Anxiety.*)

EMMA: A twinge. It's passed.

EMMA moves to the ship rails and looks out at the flying porpoises.

HENRY looks, too, and at her back.

HENRY: You move like one of them with me. Like a porpoise.

EMMA: (*Suddenly.*) I hate nature. Don't you? Fields. Bovine benevolence.

HENRY: On your way to changing into your bikini, could we get into the bunk?

The DECK STEWARD returns with a colleague, carrying a cake with one candle on it, singing 'Happy Birthday to You' and giv-ing the cake to EMMA with a knife. She cuts it.

STEWARD: (*Prim.*) The various members of your family wanted to come up to share the festivities.

What we see is suddenly crowded with the faces of HENRY'S and EMMA'S 60-year-old daughter and their middle-aged grandchildren: stylized icons of blue-haired age, with enlarged faces like gargoyles of cheeriness, lifting mugs of bouillon and eating cake.

DAUGHTER: (*With bouffant hair and a spangled eye-veil.*) Long and happy life, Mummy.

EMMA: (*To HENRY, aside.*) Help! Henry!

HENRY: How do they manage to be so depressing?

EMMA: They're not seeing us.

HENRY: Fighting off age isn't doing them any good. It can make someone decrepit, a blue rinse.

We are in the cabin. EMMA prowls around it, thinking some-thing out. Green lino, a bunk, and two small beds, a shower to the right.

EMMA: Do you know what this is? It's the ship's hospital. Look at the way the beds are nailed down. Have you got your usual hammer on you?

HENRY: Had you a deadly deed in mind on your birthday?

121

EMMA: I thought you'd enjoy doing a bit of prising. (*Pause.*) I always suspected it was the ship's hospital.

HENRY: They suggested the padded cell but it wasn't very padded. Not in the sense of quilted. Not what I'd want for you.

EMMA: Padded cell?

HENRY: They hadn't got a double cabin. Only two *separate* cabins. One was first-class and one was steerage. The assistant purser thought we shouldn't be separated. So we're here.

EMMA: (*Tugging at bed, measuring floor space and bed widths with her hand span.*) We *are* separated. These are *iron hospital beds*, nailed to the floor, three feet apart, two foot six wide. If only we could push them together, Henry? Couldn't we get them together?

HENRY lies down on the bottom layer of the bunk.

EMMA: A bunk isn't what either of us wants.

HENRY: Don't think I haven't tried.

EMMA: So you haven't got a hammer.

HENRY: Your hands are beautiful, aren't they? I noticed it for the umpteenth time when you were doing the hand-span business. I've seen you do that at the flat, measuring places for the sofa.

EMMA: It'll be nice when the flat's finished.

HENRY: It's always difficult, starting out. I'll be earning more money soon. I don't like your working so hard when I'm not bringing in anything much. I feel as if you're supporting a student taxi-driver. Geriatric taxi-driver.

EMMA: I enjoy it. (*Touches his face.*) You're not geriatric. You're Henry.

HENRY: I'm sorry I haven't got a hammer on me. I've got my Boy Scout penknife but that's bent.

EMMA: By the beds, I suppose. We're better as we are, aren't we?

HENRY: In the one bed. Do I snore?

EMMA: No, never. Sometimes you get into the middle of one of the beds and then I ask you if you could move over and then nothing happens for a while so I have a read in the chair or lie on top of you. Depending.

HENRY: When *you* get into the middle of the bed, and I ask you if you could move over, you say 'Sorry' as if you were in the underground at rush-hour, and you heave over, but somehow stay in the same place. But you're very polite. Almost courtly. (*Pause.*) Do you think I'm ever going to be the same class as you?

EMMA: Darling, it's my birthday. Don't say things like that.

HENRY: So?

EMMA: It was very sweet of you, what you said about the bed, but don't give up hope. Some day we'll have a bigger bed.

HENRY: One of us will *always* be in the middle of it.

EMMA takes off her dress, answering him through the flowered tulle folds.

EMMA: That's called determinism.

HENRY: What are you doing? I just wondered why you were getting undressed, after getting dressed, after having a shower.

EMMA: We always did things in the wrong order.

HENRY: Life?

EMMA: No. Life has been right. (*Pause.*) We'd have been better off in a single first-class cabin.

HENRY: I know, but the assistant purser's an old gentleman and he thought we'd be happier in a room together with two beds. He couldn't settle down to the idea of sharing a single bed. Not two oldies like us.

EMMA: Is that the way *he* sees us, too? (*Cries.*) Can you undo this hook for me? (*Her bra.*) I can't go on.

HENRY: One has to.

EMMA: And that steward. And our dismal progeny.

HENRY: The assistant purser was very taken with your hair.

EMMA: Really?

HENRY: He said he knew it was real. Real titian, he said. No henna.

There is a knock at the door. EMMA is naked and makes no effort to put anything on. HENRY throws a towel over her shoulders and shouts in answer to the knock.

HENRY: Come in.

The assistant purser enters with a ratty looking rug that he puts on the linoleum.

ASSISTANT PURSER: As I thought. Real titian. No henna.

ASSISTANT PURSER arranges the mat between the two beds.

ASSISTANT PURSER: A lovely bride. I brought the mat for the sake of convenience in the case of any travel between the two beds in the course of a night. (*Cockney, kindly.*) You wouldn't want to catch a cold on honeymoon.

Now HENRY is naked, seen from the back, lying beside EMMA, who is on her back.

EMMA: The years pass like fun, don't they? Race by? I can't be eighty-one. It's only other people who think we're old. Darling, that's the foot that's got gout.

HENRY: Your foot or my foot?

EMMA: In this case, I was talking about my foot.

HENRY: It's not gout you've got, it's fleas.

EMMA: Fleas? A nice thing to say to someone on honey-moon. The assistant purser thinks we're on honeymoon. So do I. So do you.

HENRY: It's because the assistant purser thinks we're on honeymoon that he brought in that ratty bit of carpet between our beds, and it's because of that ratty bit of carpet between our beds that you've got fleas.

EMMA: Why are you crawling about over me with a cake of soap? It's not good for your rheumatism.

HENRY: You know I don't have rheumatism when I'm alone with you. (*Pause.*)

EMMA: And the cake of soap?

HENRY: A wet cake of soap is the way to catch fleas.

EMMA: Where did you learn that?

HENRY: In the war.

EMMA: Which war?

HENRY: There've been so many.

EMMA: You've been away so many times, but you've al-ways come back. What luck! (*She cries.*)

HENRY: Why do you cry when you're happy?

EMMA: You'll get used to it. There's ages more to get through.

HENRY: Thank goodness.

EMMA: There's nothing to be frightened of. We're not ele-phants. Elephants are said to have delicious sensations from being frightened about nothing.

EMMA goes into the shower. HENRY follows her with the cake of soap. We can see her through the white shower curtains: a misty glimpse, like a Bonnard.

EMMA: How old are we?

HENRY: One hundred and sixty-four. Our combined age, you mean. There's plenty of time.

DAME OF THE BRITISH EMPIRE, BBC

IT's extraordinary that they didn't get B.H.," said Yseult, an actress with elocution famous all over England. If only Wilde were still alive to write for her, radio listeners said. If only Congreve.

"B.H.?" said Bell, the young pregnant wife of the assistant producer. She had not yet grown used to the reign of initials at the BBC. The D.G. was the Director-General. She had once been engaged to the D.O.P.S., the Director of Overseas Programme Services. Baffled by him, though already keenly missing their future, she talked to the vicar and cancelled the wedding time reserved at the church.

Yseult, D.B.E. (Dame of the British Empire), sipped her wine. "B.H., dear. Broadcasting House. From the air, the roof is the shape of a battleship. Obviously the easiest point for a crucial direct hit. They got a great deal of Harley Street. But B.H. carried on. I remember the miracle of it, even though I was only a small child."

The second great actress at this dinner party was called Nora, also a D.B.E. The dinner, an anxious one, was at a refectory table in a house of wood and glass beside an inlet of the Thames near Henley. Nora said, "Yes, I remember. I was in the Wrens. I hadn't thought of you as being a child in the Blitz, Yseult."

"You *remember?*" said Yseult. "I've only really heard about it. From my father, who was on fire duty. My little nose pressed against the windowpane in Portland Place. I couldn't sleep. I've never been an easy sleeper." ("No, you haven't," her husband had said long ago, after banishment to the dressing room. Now dead, she thought, and I still upright, Lord help us.)

The two actresses were famous through the world for a radio duologue between haughty mistress and fast-thinking maid that was broadcast not only in England every week but also on the BBC World Service. Their enunciation was so clear, their writer so direct, that their soothed listeners in Africa flooded them with particularly devoted fan letters.

Yseult pursued the point about being old enough to recall the Blitz. She had been placed, at the last minute, at the head of the table, where the famous elocutory boom that gave sound engineers weekly trouble could do no particular harm to the people seated next to her: the obeisant assistant producer and the gentle, grey-haired head of drama, who knew the value of the series and the pitfalls of his actresses' pairing. At the foot of the table was the writer of the series, their host: a good cook, hostile to blenders and serf to a sieve.

The duo of Yseult and Nora worked on the air as it never could have done onstage. Yseult, who at six had changed her name from her baptismal one, Ann, because she thought the Arthurian motif fit for her, now stood six foot three. Possible for a character part, hard for a heroine. For ten years she had worked in opera, but her height made things difficult. The tenors with her wore the highest possible lifts inside their boots, but they still stood well below her. Costume designers always gave her long skirts, and she would sing with her knees bent; there grew into being so many cruel imitations of her Groucho walk that she was stricken. The last scald of fate's revenge came when she was singing in *La Sonnambula* and the bridge in the sleepwalking scene failed to break as it should have. The stage manager wondered whether to bring down the curtain. The conductor dithered. She led the orchestra, sang more, walked back, and tried the stage trickery again. Again the bridge didn't break. Music critics in the audience started to laugh. The third time it worked, and she fell safely, to the relief of the insurance company, who were being telephoned by the money-minded director of the opera house. Her noble common sense in this notorious opera debacle, practised by a prima donna thought to be unmitigatedly vain, went uncommended. Her pride had been scraped, but she took action of a mildness not attributed to her. Only one other person at the table knew what she had achieved: the writer and host had been there. To the others, including the kindly Nora, no Ibsen door-banger, she was as she had always seemed: invulnerably sure of herself and prone to the stupidity that often goes with competitiveness.

So. Yseult at the head of the table, hastily placed there instead of at her host's right, so that she could lead the table in general without doing harm in the particular; Nora on the host's right; the host, tall, witty, with long legs that tangled like poles in a ski fall; the assistant producer; his wife, Bell, already feeling her own hand in her lap as separate from herself, as if the baby.

"Have some more of this curious stew," said the host.

"Curious it is," said Yseult. "In the vein of farce, as the cuisine modes go."

"Yseult," said Nora. "He had to cook for one person on the Scarsdale Diet, one person allergic to dairy products, one vegetarian, one person who swells up on anything farinaceous. So we might have had a hot-pot of polyunsaturated margarine and fresh basil and turnip broth, wouldn't you say?"

"How are your cows?" said the pregnant girl with true interest.

"Well, darling," said Nora, "we haven't had the right weather this year, so we've only been getting twenty gallons from the ones who usually give us thirty. So we've got to be patient until they have calves again next year and lactate again. It's the one thing we can't blame on the recession."

"I was thinking about them," said Bell.

Nora turned to her. "Yes. I've moved from the house, you know. After Billy's death it was too big. So I switched to one of the dairyman's cottages. My daughter called it the Old Cow's House and I thought it was funny at first, but now it makes me feel old. I hope a sense of humour doesn't pass, like the capacity to do backbends."

"Can you do backbends?" said the assistant producer. "Or could you?"

"Now only if I use a wall or a doorjamb." Nora made a "May I?" face at her host and did a backbend down the doorjamb of the door behind the open-plan kitchen, the house within being architect-designed and short of doors.

Bell clapped. Yseult said, "Wonderfully achieved." She could have made "Hello" sound like a full line of Racine, if such a word had been in his vocabulary. She and Nora had played together for so long, with a warmth and ease owed mostly to Nora's sunny well-being, that not many people around even this table knew that the quick sophistications plied between the two great actresses playing domestic-serial situations in Restoration style emanated as much from Yseult as from Nora, or that Yseult was fighting for something. Her life, you could say.

"I noticed you didn't have the ratatouille on the sundeck," said the host.

"I don't care for a first course away from table," said Yseult.

"I like the garlic in it, and the Pernod, was it? An invention? Garlic makes you sleep without dreams," said Nora.

"Garlic makes you unknowable," said the assistant producer. He was frightened by having spoken, but sped on.

"The first smell of garlic comes through the soles of naked feet. Been known since Roman times. You can tell from the amount of foot-washing in the Gospels that Jesus' feet smelt." He had a drink of wine, and said, "Shortest verse in the Bible: 'Jesus stank.' "

There was a pause of horror. "Dear heart," said Yseult, putting her arthritic but beautiful hand on his, "that remark is at the level of graffiti. It's a level not up to your instep."

There was a glance between Yseult and Nora, and Nora said, "Do you remember the mess we made about the poetry reading?"

"All too well. You may tell it. Except that the mess, the *confusione,* was not made by us. It was in the passive, not the active. The mess was made."

"We were asked to give a poetry reading at a car factory," said Nora, "by a young man full of purpose about bringing poetry to the people." She paused, not laughing, which was her habit when she found herself absurd for being trapped in the jargon of liberalism. She had been chased out of a job in Hollywood because she caught the note of Fascism rising in the anti-Semitism there long before most people had picked up the wavelength. "Yseult and I were to do a lunchtime recital. At this car factory. We made a new translation of 'The Wife of Bath' to lift their spirits."

"Very little of valuable lewdness has been written for many a century. Of true value. Not pinchbeck. Don't you agree?" said Yseult to the table at large. "Now, this table itself, being of the monastic, reminding us of the ethos of Mt. Athos, tells us everything about what we now think of as puritanism and therefore, of course, of its obverse or antithesis, which is to say the lewd in its own pure, though scarcely puritanical, sense.''

"I don't understand a word you're saying," said the assistant producer.

"No," said the host.

"I have read in Middle English many times in the desert throughout Africa, and the people of the sand have clustered to hear. Have understood me," said Yseult. "At the car factory I would have been understood, Nora. It was simply the absence of the people that was at fault.''

"Darlings," said Nora, "this nice young man was perfectly a Socialist, but brought up in Bournemouth, and educated at a quite expensive preparatory school before Modern Greats at Oxford, and he picked us up for a lunchtime recital at twenty to one and when we arrived the canteen was quite empty. For this friend of the people didn't know that his people's lunch hour is from twelve to one. If one starts work at seven, you see. He needed comfort for his mistake, but he only eats yogurt. Other people's yogurt. He believes in being badly off.''

"Easily achieved by not working," said the host.

Yseult suddenly found the chronicle of the gaffe not funny and said to her host, "You told us that last episode was going to be repeated. I've thought of what to do about the lines that don't get the laughs from the studio audience. So odd. A dowager of the highest rank saying to her butler after a line from her friend, myself, 'In a crisis of lethargy one does not speak at one's best from a hammock.' Now, in the night I hit on it. We shall get the laugh if we reverse the lines. The preceding line, intentionally dulled of course to lead up to the next, should be spoken by Nora. The response, I take it over, and we have our effect.''

"The laugh," said Bell.

"A question of collaborative creation," said Yseult. "By displacement we perfect."

"So who does get the laugh who didn't get the laugh?" said Bell.

"Dumper dumper dumper dum," hummed the assistant producer in warning, nodding to the head of the table.

The head of drama said he felt sure something of the sort would work out well on the floor. Head of drama not for nothing, he diverted and said, "Children write to us. A lot of them. One was invited to a studio audience and I had a long letter from him in the Gothic script."

Yseult said, drawing the letter from her bag, "Yes, I should say it was Gothic."

Nora said, "He sent me a carbon copy," and also drew it from her bag. "You read it, Yseult. I think the boy had been reading a lot. The letter is from Brixton."

Yseult used a lorgnette on an ivory handle and read aloud, " 'My dear Dames Yseult and Nora: Notwithstanding the lateness of this apology for my absence at your programme, I hope it is still a valid one. The cause of the lateness in question was the bloody (pardon me) tube. I had left my home at approximately 2:25 P.M., knowing that a journey to the BBC would not consume the greatest interval of time. I waited a bit and boarded an exceptionally filthy compartment. When I had arrived at the Oxford Circus halt, I was stalled in the train for some time. Estimating that I would arrive at the performance while it had already commenced, I decided not to do so and left the stranded compartment. I then directed my steps out of the station and professed to myself that I would walk home since I delight in walking. On reaching home, I decided to give an explanation to you both that very evening but neglected doing thus. For the past week or so, I have neglected my obligation to you, I regretfully must pray.' " Yseult paused.

"I think it's 'say,' " said Nora.

" 'Pray' is a funnier mischance from a prodigiously gifted young mind." Yseult carried on, " 'In any event, that is all I have to expound to you on that matter. It will interest you to know that I have finished *Wuthering Heights,* which made quite a signet on my emotions for its passion and different faces of human nature.' "

"Facets," said Nora, forgetting that Yseult had trouble now with her eyes. "He deserves attention, darling."

Yseult went on, " 'Though I am making tentative arrangements concerning a gathering, to which you are of course invited, I would like to find occasion for meeting with you prior to the aforementioned gathering. My timetable for daily activity is exceedingly flexible: much of my days are spent at home. I know that you and I will have much to chat about for an afternoon's tête-à-tête. My heartfelt wishes to you. Yours ever, Nathaniel Fare.' "

Bell clapped. The head of drama, used to whisking away attention from an act impossible to counteract, said, "May I tell the table a story about you, Yseult? It caused great trouble to O.B."

"Outside Broadcasts," said the assistant producer.

"Now, many of you will have wondered what happened to our great Yseult when she dropped opera."

"The bridge incident. So I got married," said Yseult, playing with a fork.

"To a farmer in Lincolnshire," said Nora.

"We were married for six years."

"So you *must* remember the Blitz," said the host, as lightly as he could.

"I've lied about my age so often I don't know how old I am any longer, in truth," said Yseult. "What a pleasure: linen table napkins. A picnic laid on napery upon the greensward."

"Who said that?" asked the host.

"Yseult did," said Nora, giving time.

The head of drama went on, "We were doing our 'Farmer's Weekly' programme. Our breakfast programme each week, live. A farm breakfast at six-thirty in the morning because of the milking. We arrived, and the sound effects of teaspoons and cereal were excellent. We spoke easily of pigs, arable-land value, value-added tax for farmers, clay and iron content, the enviable Lincolnshire soil. Yseult was pouring tea, and to my shame I didn't recognize her inherent greatness. But there was a fine white wall and I told our excellent cameraman to put a rustic chair against it with Yseult, given her permission, upon it. We—I speak for the unit—wanted her contribution as a farmer's obviously hardworking wife. Our interviewer said that she must find the life very interesting. Do you remember what you said, Yseult?"

"Of course."

"What was it?"

" '*I hate it.*' That's what I said."

"We couldn't bleep it."

"I had to go on after that. My husband had taken the car keys from me, I said, in case I ran away."

"And then?" said the host.

"I went to the railway station after the programme on my child's bicycle, and came to London to find a job. My child was better in the country and she loved her father."

"How much money did you have?" said Bell.

"The stationmaster took the bicycle as credit for a ticket. I should imagine him to have been a man of the calibre to send the bicycle back somehow. I slept in Regent's Park. One of our Edwardian summers." Yseult played with her napkin, and took out her compact to hide her tears, using the napkin to blow her nose: an action observed by every-one. "That wretched agriculture has left me in a permanent state of flu," she said. "I wish our sound-effects man were here for me to pay him tribute. When we hear our play-backs, I have never detected my having a blocked nose. It would be a vulgar comic device for my character. That young man has perfect pitch for the self-absorption that is the tonic note of comedy." But no one found it funny that she was absorbed by her elegant nose, the nose of a Plantag-enet with adenoids.

ON EACH
OTHER'S
TIME

"ARE YOU AS LOW as I am?" said Alfred Rowlett, aged thirty-four, yelling cheerfully on the telephone from Bolivia at eight-thirty-five in the morning.

"I don't know how low that is," shouted his brother Federico (born in Positano but English as they come), aged thirty-two, from Madras, where it was five past six in the evening.

"About the riots," said Alfred.

"Where you are or where I am?" said Federico.

"In Liverpool," said Alfred.

"Probably lower, though I'm more resilient," said Federico. He was at the perennial disadvantage of being younger, a disadvantage that unduly weighed on him, because it was by nature unmendable. This insistence on being the more resilient was a perpetual defence. "I can hear your breakfast coming in."

"That isn't breakfast, that's my bed. They don't do

breakfast here. They bring the bed instead. I suppose so that they don't have to make it, because it's gone again in the evening. I have to sleep on the floor. I have to wait for the bed to come back again in the morning and tip them, because otherwise they make a mess of my notes."

"You must be flaked."

"No, there's a rush on and not having a bed saves time. Is it tiring there?"

"I don't seem to be sleeping."

"Try lying down," said Alfred. "You never remember that part. No one can sleep standing up except horses."

"The thing is, I have to walk about from now on so as to be up for being woken. They do it about ten at night here if you order a wake-up knock for four in the morning. I think it's because the English were so fierce to Indians about unpunctuality for nearly two hundred years that we've made them nervous."

"Have you got the figures yet?"

Federico read out to Alfred facts about divorce costs printed in an article published in London. They were about alimony, maintenance, the rising rates to any harried and/or married citizen in a string of countries that had nothing to do with where either of them was and nothing to do with England either. This was the way the brothers often helped each other. They were both social cartoonists, working at their drawing boards and listening in far-flung places to dilemmas and gripes expressed through many a beard net or yashmak, and their notions were kin. All four in this generation of the family alone were working wits of one sort or another. They had early come to an agreement about pooling information on their offices' foreign telephone expenses. The method saved money on long-winded explanations to researchers in London, who were anyway no good at pulling together suspiciously obscured facts even when they smelled as high as rank herring; it also saved the tedium of being put on hold with a caption for a cartoon and then cut off after someone at a news desk said, "Hang on while I get a pencil."

Alfred, the eldest of the four, was a specialist now on Latin America. He had been drawing cartoon chronicles ever since Oxford, with a wit in the tradition of pamphleteers and broadsheet writers, about the doings of the flag-wagging "peacemakers" in high office whom he found in most countries of the world. He and Federico, the brother closest to him, had in common an unusual lack of careerism. Federico was the more solid man, as the saying goes, but no Rowlett was dulled. He had high degrees in divorce law. His knowledge about infidelity in the countries of the world had brought him to a unique point in financial cartooning.

When Federico was born, already named, it was pointed out to their lucid father that Alfred's and Federico's Christian names would render them both Freds. "*Render?*" said Mark Rowlett. "Render down, as with lard, or render to, as with bills? No child of ours is ever going to be nicknamed." Being a satirist, he had no need to raise his voice. "To be fair, two Oxford friends have made the same point. But if anyone really wants to collapse into lingo, the boys can be Alf and Fred. Though over my live body."

147

Mark Rowlett in his married life had always lived somewhere in Cumberland. He had moved and moved, with his
shortwave radio and a very old Remington, on which he
typed articles and broadcasts. His wife, Constance, was
a theoretical mathematician, a wool-embroiderer, and a
breeder of local sheep providing the best wool. Her third
child was Deirdre, a beautiful young woman of twenty-eight
engaged in a series of prodigiously long and wry articles—
wry in a dodgy way, dodging you for fifty columns of sobre
type every time—about trees' ecology on this planet. She
lived mostly in Scandinavia at the moment, for the interest
of the trees. She, too, was on the economical family plan of
research shared by telephone. Her childhood had been lone-
some, though Alfred earnestly looked after her. A lot of her
time had been spent in counting trees, much as other children make list upon list of friends, but the tree familiars had
been so often lost to her by the family moves that she early
despaired of anything's having longevity, including study
and species. Long before she had got distinctions in every
Oxford matriculation subject, she got below nought at
school in Scripture, deportment, tolerance, and basketwork.
No one in the family was inclined to take this seriously, but
her father, an investigative reporter, investigated. He found
that the basketwork mistress was also the Scripture mistress, and that for two terms running an embarrassed Deirdre had been made to play Eve, lamenting Adam's torn rib
between the school desks. After that discovery Mark took
her away from school and taught her himself. They worked
swiftly together and she well on her own. Whichever house

they were living in at the time, there was the same Carolean chair behind the desk where she was allowed to spread books for classics, which they saved for the evening. The chair's ribbed legs left marks on her own, because she twisted them around the carving.

The youngest, twenty-four, was Peter, a tall, thin boy who became stroke of his university boat and a half-blue at squash. As a child, when at long last he had begun to speak, he was loquacious whenever lonely. His mother saw that he felt apart from the older three. He even loathed food, this skinny lad, while the rest of the table merely found food the least interesting thing at any dinner. If ever he had to be mildly punished for not doing homework, the only punish-ment meted was to shut him away at his desk in his own unlocked room. Quite unresentful, he cancelled out the punishment by going immediately to sleep under the desk, his thin complex of limbs like coils of plumbing under a basin. Constance found a clue when he said out of nowhere that he felt underexercised, "like a dozy lion, the dangerous kind." She immediately took him rowing every dawn on Lake Derwent Water. She was a good oar herself, for rea-sons no one knew. Like Peter, she was left-handed, but she gave the left oar to him to lend him a sporting chance. At eight, he didn't notice this, but at eight and a half he did. Thinking to repay her in effort, he taught himself shorthand secretly at his coed school, though the girls scoffed. As soon as he left school he became a cub reporter in the dock dis-tricts of Northumberland and Durham. The loquacity ended and he became inquiring, with the reporter's gift of seeming invisible. It came, perhaps, like all the children's distinct talents, from one or the other of their parents. Peter's conciseness came very much from his laconic father.

Mark's fame as a satirist had begun at Oxford in the days of the Spanish Civil War. He was to speak at the Union against an undergraduate named Hogg, whose political views he very much disliked. Mark let loose a greased hog in the hall. He had since been trying to explain to his Oxford contemporaries that a greased hog is not satire. Prewar Oxford was a curious interlude in his life. Brawn, beefy minds, a lot of sunrise baying for lukewarm Chablis left over from someone's party the night before. His County Durham childhood, in Consett, had been poor and frightening. His seaman father was drowned when Mark was nine, an only child; at the age of twelve he was seen off to sit for a scholarship to Winchester. He went alone through the ticket barrier carrying a cello left to him by his father. It was bigger than he was, and the weight added to the twitchings in his kneecaps. Despite fear he got a scholarship. After that one bullish year at Oxford, also on a scholarship, he joined up, in the Merchant Navy. Unwarlike, decorated for bravery three times when his ships were torpedoed, and still wondering whether he shouldn't have stood trial as a conscientious objector and chosen the hated option of sugar-beet farming, he went back to postwar Oxford. What an Oxford. British-railways buffet sort of meals instead of dinners in Hall, men too old and grieved to be undergraduates trying desperately to make up the war years they had lost. Mark threw in his hand after two terms and started to earn a living as an apprentice typesetter up North. Then he married Constance and added to his wages by proofreading the telephone directory.

"To think there was a time when I proofed it," he said out loud.

"What, darling?" said Constance, peering in at his study window from the garden.

"And now I can't even see well enough to find it."

"What?"

"The telephone directory."

"I put it away the last time the phone was cut off." The quarterly, laggardly, unpaid phone bills were the insistent reason—professional habit, family links—for the many moves. The moves were distressing to Mark because of his stacks of references and distressing to Constance as a sheep breeder. Mark never had more than a penny, though he worked all the time.

"We must be able to phone," he said, as usual, though as if the point had just occurred. "I've got to keep in touch."

"You've got your shortwave radio."

"That's incoming. I've got to have a two-way system, don't you see. Bring me my chequebook and we'll be honest citizens."

"We're overdrawn."

"We can always sell something."

"What?"

Mark looked around him. "We could flog the complete Galsworthy. And there are plenty of other books I could be

151

without by now. Haven't we got a load of things somewhere about Iceland?"

"Iceland? Wouldn't they be Deirdre's?"

"No. A friend of mine in the Big Apple wrote to me a
while ago and happened to mention that there's an enormous Iceland section in a perfectly normal bookshop on Fifth
Avenue. Colossal. Far bigger than all the European sections
put together, he said. Which proves that there must be a
mounting scholarly demand for commentaries on the Edda.
Possibly, though not necessarily, even for the Edda itself.
Sensing my interest, this kind chap sent me five feet of books
about Iceland in return for some valueless tips about gold in-
gots. A solemn man. Illiterate, sadly. From a business magazine called *Know Your Capitalism*. Keen-nosed and a worker
at heart, he detected a bookish man when he saw one and
sent me these five feet. They must be somewhere."

"You could inscribe them with your name and that would
add to the value. I'm told that the place to do it is on the
title page, never on the inside cover."

"How did you find that out?"

"I was asking an antiquarian bookseller I happened to
meet in the fishmonger's."

"Great. And you could sell some of your tapestry chair
backs. They're great stuff. I'd help you fix up a show."

"They're not up to snuff, Mark. Not yet."

"Then I'll sell my old atlas."

"Not that one. It's the one with the marine map glued
into it." Mark, by one of the many accidents that cling to
childbirth and to seafaring parents, had been born on a Brit-

ish boat accidentally storm-tossed into someone else's fishing rights. This, he insisted, made him either a British diplomat entitled to a *laissez-passer* or an anarchist. Mark warmed to the idea of V.I.P. travel all over the world with no official rude enough to look at any of his passports (which happened, for brave and honourable reasons, to be forged) or, better still, made him a free port in human form, with the privilege of duty-free Scotch.

After a moment of meditation on that, he waved his hand at Constance and said, "Well, sell your car then."

"It wouldn't fetch a penny." She was certainly the only person in the family or at the local garage who could drive it. "Besides, I use it to *save* money on the telephone calls I'd otherwise have to make to get shops to deliver."

Constance was an excellent driver of this car, changing gears tirelessly to coax it up to its maximum speed of twenty-four miles an hour, uniquely knowledgeable about opening the boot. Even her athletic sons couldn't kick or prise a way into it when they wanted to carry their luggage into the house after she had driven slowly to Newcastle to meet a plane from Guatemala or China. The back seat was piled high with wool-embroidered canvases on their way to the furniture-maker. Constance, a chain smoker, had often been noticed using her cigarette as the ignition key at the first attempt to start.

"Not that the telephone's my medium," said Mark, "but we never know when there mightn't be an editor ringing about a typo, or a film producer, or the children. I can always tell when it's going to be them. Only thing that makes me believe in God, or gods, is when old planchette starts ringing and I know it's one of them. Talking of God, darling, we really did have them in an abhorrently monarchical order. First a boy heir, then another boy as backup, then a girl who's probably going to keep the monarchy going for good in this age of Women's Lib and Queens by being the first woman on the moon, then yet another boy in case there's ever need of a dauphin if the others kick the bucket before me. Do you remember a particularly territorialist *Henry V,* where the Dauphin was a very small old man playing with a yo-yo?''

"Mark, that's got no connection with Peter at all. He was only small, ever, when he was a baby, and he only played with a yo-yo when he was a baby. Babies *are* small and they *do* play with yo-yos.''

"He didn't open his mouth until he was four. The others were reading by two and a half.''

"He talked enough to the other children. The youngest in families often do that.''

"He's certainly shot up since,'' Mark said. "And spoken up. I've cut out a great piece he did this morning. It's on your dressing table. I couldn't find anything by any of the others, could you?''

"There's a nice reference to Alfred in *The Economist.* Quoting him.''

"Signs of dangerous radical infiltration in *The Economist* at last. Great. I've *never* made *The Economist.*''

By selling Galsworthy, the five Icelandic feet, and a sheep by Landseer, Constance had the phone reconnected. Mark

was sitting by his shortwave radio as usual, straight to work
in his dressing gown from shaving, monitoring events in Ulster, Poland, and Albania, when the engineers came.

"Constance," he said, in the quiet voice she always
heard.

One of the engineers said that he'd seen Mrs. Rowlett
going out in her car. Then he himself left. Mark knew both
engineers well. They were named Frank and Vic. They had
been many times to disconnect and reconnect this telephone.

"Engineers and handymen and carpenters and American
policemen always travel in pairs, don't they?" said Mark.
"Where's Vic gone?"

"He's parking the van."

"Hard to find a place to park these days in the country,"
said Mark, looking out of his window at the deserted land-
scape.

Frank fiddled for a time, did the wiring, and then dipped
into his back trouser pocket for a piece of paper. "I wonder if
you could give me a bit of advice about this," he said.

Mark read carefully. It was a pop lyric written out in pencil. "I'm glad you did this. It's the real stuff, I should say.
Have you got a tune in mind?"

"I'm known for my whistling, but I'm not satisfied with
the last two lines. I want to say 'stygian' at the end of the
seventh line, but I can't hit on a rhyme for the eighth."

Mark gave the matter his complete attention. He stood
up, with a little difficulty because of a twinge of arthritis,
and for the first time in years managed to get a grasp on a

thesaurus that underpinned the whole wobbling pile of the Oxford English Dictionary. Mark and Frank worked on the problem.

Frank rejected many possibilities and then seized on one. "That'll do it." He started to whistle. "Yes. I can hear that. Very nice of you."

"I didn't know you did this."

"You've got to have another skill, haven't you. With un-employment." Frank started to pick up his tools.

Mark thought, and then said, "Vic's not back yet?"

"If you're interested, I'll just show you what I've done." Frank unscrewed the telephone so that the conglomeration of wires was exposed. "I cleaned it up for you, because they don't dust much in the instrument shop, not secondhand telephones." The telephone bell then rang, surprising Mark from this phone offal. Frank said, "Receiving. Dry cleaner's, pickup at Mrs. Fawcett, she's all right, she won't mind the other pickups. Going to lunch, no trouble. Deliveries before we pick her up again, pack that little lot in easily before the corroded jack at Ridleys. Roger."

"So Vic uses the van as a taxi while you're working," said Mark. Frank nodded, and Mark said, "Very sensible. It's what you were saying yourself about writing songs."

"Two strings to your bow now if you're going to have half a chance. My dad used to say that, but he never had the opportunity. As a miner. That's your telephone this time. I'll be off."

"Keep at it," said Mark. He let the telephone ring once more, said firmly to himself that he wasn't getting the plan-

156

chette signal, but wasn't in time to stop himself from saying into the telephone gaily, "Not by any chance a family conclave?" He responded with just as much alacrity to the reply, from an editor who wanted a long piece in a hurry. Mark was not a man to live by one hope alone.

"Your phone was out of order for days," said the editor.

"I hadn't paid the bill."

"Can you do the piece by Friday?"

"That's late for you. Thursday."

"Telephone it in. Reverse the charge. Many thanks. Make the copytakers read it back if you want. You use a lot of difficult names. In good spirits, are you, apart from the news?"

"Not much apart from news now, a lot of people say, but with the amount of activity that's just been going on privately in this house, I should say there was a good deal else. Fighting off unemployment on all fronts up here."

"Write about that next time, if you would?"

"Maybe. If I could." Mark started at once to make notes for the immediate piece. As usual, the notes were made in his head.

A young girl who lived in the house rent-free in return for helping Constance with the sheep came into his study in tears. "I can't stand the life here. I can't get things happening. I don't like letting Constance down, but I want to pack straightaway. I need a lot of your old newspapers for my packing boxes. They're full of earth, because we had them for the rhododendrons. I'm sorry, but I'm going to be nineteen in a month. I've maybe still got a future, haven't I? And it isn't here." Crying most bitterly, she started to pick up piles of his carefully sorted newspapers and magazines, which stood in high stacks all around the room and on his sofa.

"You can't have those. They're work." Mark got up without the usual difficulty and put his arm around her shoulders, walking slowly to the door in his dressing gown and carpet slippers. "It'll be all right. You have to go by your instinct. Now, lining the boxes. I think we could snitch a lot of drawer-lining paper for you from the kitchen cupboards. You look in the bedrooms and I'll ransack the kitchen."

"Mrs. Rowlett will mind. I can't call her Constance any longer."

"She's very fond of you, but people have to move on."

"I meant about having to buy new lining paper. Even you haven't got enough to manage on, and you're clever and you've been at it for years. I've probably left it too late already." She ran upstairs, not looking back, shouting, "It comes of being self-employed, does it? But I can't think of anything else. A delivery girl or a waitress, if I could get it, and then something of my own in the evenings."

Mark went on stripping the kitchen of lining paper for her.

Without his knowing it, all of his children were due to arrive in Newcastle from their points abroad. And without telling him, Constance had gone off by car to collect them. They arrived at home, Constance taking out her cigarette to beam at the success of her surprise. Talk; private talk between Mark and Constance about the girl upstairs; questions; sandwiches of dressed crab.

"A binge," said Mark, eating little.

"What's the noun for someone who binges?" said Federico.

"It couldn't be 'binger.' If you read it, that would make it rhyme with 'singer,' " said Deirdre.

"Why not with 'harbinger'?" said Constance.

"Anyway, it would never in a million years describe Mark," said Federico. "He's the family skeleton. The skeleton in all our cupboards."

"None of us, not one of us, could ever aspire to be as disreputable as he is," said Alfred in homage. "What's all this about the girl upstairs?"

"Not girl. Mary. She's worried about going to seed," said Constance.

"What does she do?" said Deirdre.

"Helps Constance with the sheep," said Mark. "She plants grass with more natural vitamins in it. More natural than usual in Cumberland."

"Then going to seed would be an endemic worry," said Alfred.

"No. It's endemic to being nineteen stuck in the country with unemployment getting worse. Her brother in Newcastle has just been laid off," said Mark.

"So she's quitting," said Constance. "And now she's concerned about leaving us in the lurch on top of everything else."

"One thing always comes of another, that's what I always say," said Peter, with for him an unusual note of the Rowlett high spirits that were sometimes taken by the envious or the inattentive for callousness.

There was a family pause, each wondering about the others' doings.

Alfred stripped off his shirt and heaved some new rocks from a nearby cliff to improve the run of the garden waterfall. Federico looked after the departing girl and carried her boxes to the bus stop two by two. Deirdre went to work, lying down on her bed. Peter and his mother went to the nearest shops to buy food and to drop Mark's oldest jacket at the dry cleaner's. Mark started to work. Old touch typist that he was, he didn't bother to turn on his desk lamp. He worked for five or six hours, finished, switched on the lamp, and went to edit his top copy. He couldn't see anything typed on it at all. Fifteen pages, and nothing there. Hands shaking, he tried every pair of spectacles he had. There was no doubt. The thing he most dreaded for himself had happened. He leaned back to think. I must leap into my life, but I'm falling through a skylight in the blackout, someone was leading me and they didn't tell me it wasn't floor, I must leap into my life if it cuts me to splinters, I must think of something else to do but there's nothing but read and write that I want to do. My face feels slashed to bits, I wonder if I did that when I was shaving and just didn't notice. Because I didn't notice that I couldn't see. One wouldn't, with something like shaving. He said, loudly, "Deirdre?"

Her room was opposite his study, and she came in quickly.

"I've gone blind. I've got to reconstruct a piece for a deadline. Do we know anybody who could take it down?"

Deirdre came over to look at his typewriter. She tried a few sentences standing up and told him that he could dictate to her, to go straight onto the typewriter. "Sit down. Take your time."

"I'm better if I walk about. I wouldn't know what to do with my hands and legs." He strode around with his fingers pressed against his eyeballs. His fingers had always had a way of turning back a little at the last joint, but now, when he was trying to push his eyes away, the angle was much sharper than usual. Deirdre rolled a sheet of typing paper into the machine to practise, used as she was to electric typewriters.

"Daddy," she said, "don't you realise? You had it fixed at blank. The ribbon control. It's on the place that doesn't print. It's the one for cutting stencils." Then she looked around the desk and saw, on the left, the uncollated pile of carbons that Mark, old professional that he was, had automatically made of each page.

Mark said nothing about his eyesight and only "What a piece of luck" about the carbons.

"Have you only got one bit of carbon paper? This is like lace."

"But can you read the sense?"

"I'll retype it and ask as I go. How much time have we got?"

"An hour."

They worked together fast. She said she wanted to give him time to make changes and would retype it if he wanted. It was a piece with a wide span. "I'll do it again when you've read it," she said, handing it to him.

"No, you'd better read it to me, as I'm blind," he said, so concentrated about what he had been writing in his mind that he had already accepted calamity. The old pro, though, working in another part of his head, started to read. "Mistake. I can see after all."

"You didn't notice the carbons?"

"Bloody carbons. Very good of you. I'll read the thing by the window. I'm fed up with that desk lamp. It looks like a ship's hospital. Round the Horn, steerage."

She left him alone. He said "Great" as she left. It was one of his words. He worked, telephoned the long piece, listened to his shortwave radio, and then sat back to think awhile. The thinking led to a note. Typed.

Dear Mary,

 I am sending this to you at the YWCA because that's where you said you would be, though I sensed hankerings after the YMCA. I suggest that you get in touch with a cousin of mine (male), no more decrepit than I am, who would put you up on the instant, gratis. He lives in Gosforth, and the telephone number is 2341618. He will guess immediately that you are a friend of mine, because you are asking for something free. Anyone else who calls him up is dunning him for unpaid bills or trying to deliver subpoenas about axe murders. He stands firm in the face of all such lugubrious calls, but yours will be cheerful and responded to.

His name is Bodkin Rowlett, poor chap. Take him a bottle of a vile drink called absinthe, which he likes because he associates it with literature and the French Revolution. Send the bill to me and I shall recompense you when you next come out here.

Which brings me smoothly to my next point: that you must be missing the sheep. Alfred seems to think that he is Mr. Atlas, for reasons unfounded in my eyes. He has been heaving up a large number of hideous Cumbrian stones of exorbitant size that were impeding the spread of Constance's whole-wheat-germ sheep grass. I should value your alliance in heaving them back again. When you come, and I suggest the weekend after next, dig up anything that you think would grow in Gosforth. I doubt whether anything much flourishes in the YWCA.

I forgot to tell you that I went blind today but it turned out to be a technical hitch.

It's a lousy job, job-hunting, and you don't even get paid for it. I did it myself for four years and the situation wasn't nearly as bad then. But set the alarm every day, get out there, call reverse charge whenever in need of sheepish news. And no fear.

Love,
Mark

PURSE

THE NATIONAL PURSE is shortly to be in fine fettle, our
good-looking economists agree. Right-wing, of course.
Right-wingers always agree. Well, my particular purse
is in poor shape. I am apparently what they call a bag woman,
I realised from a word-quiz on the BBC one Sunday, though I
have never thought of myself as one. Widow, yes, godmother,
yes, Sunday painter of our park life, yes, perpetual carrier of
your wedding-present bag, yes, indeed. But it seems that the
phrase has sprung into new meaning, not at all prodigal. Not,
one hopes, to be entertained for long.

You remember a happier Sunday in the park when the
wedding-present that you bought me in Florence leapt into
another role, yes, certainly another role entirely. We were
by the lake with all the local children skimming about in
little rubber-sided row boats doing no harm to a soul. A uniformed lady with a megaphone was standing on the shore
and shouting "Come in at once if not sooner, Number 15;

and Number 3, you are going to bump into Number 21 if you don't stop that racing; Number 7, I've warned you before, and Number 5 as well, about going anti-clockwise," and you walked round to the uniformed lake-sergeant-major and asked her whether she would be kind enough to look at the lightbulbs in my bag (a big bag, verging on a grip for train travel) to check whether Woolworth's had given us three 60-watt bulbs and two 100-watt bulbs or the other way around. The task was done in a chatty enough manner and the interlude on the lake was blithe. So the bag served well: my bag, so your bag, heretofore and to wit.

But I am still not a bag woman. No, begging the pardon of the Queen's English, this does not describe your bag, the bag you gave to me; nor I, not a woman, but your wife, by name, also given to me. Heretofore and to wit.

I am not especially keen on bags in general, except on Gladstone bags in which babies might have been nurtured, or as a carrier of things such as my magnifying reading spectacles, most useful to those on the watch for potholes. I don't like potholes so I keep my eyes lowered when I am walking along a pavement (or a sidewalk), no matter, no matter, what difference is there between a lift and an elevator and vertical escalated computerised transportation these unplain days. What difference is there as long as they work.

This applying only to the occasions when I have to take such a means. I prefer to remain on the ground, rock or mud though it may be.

When I was small I had a nanny and she said that you could always tell a lady by her accessories. Well, my feet have shortened with the times but I can stuff the toes with any old piece of rag to hand and the Italian leather ("an investment") still lasts. And as to my gloves, they're a goner, but who cares. And as to my bag, it has lasted me ever since Debenham and Freebody went downhill.

As you see, it is on bags that I find the mind dwelling, ridiculously taking sanctuary, and uncommanded to boot, in the violent midst of the events into which we are presently propelled. Only in the Yellow Book days did one hear, or read, of *hand*bags. A girl had a bag and a woman had a bag. Handbags were to bags what lingerie is to underclothes. Shop-sign talk, stinking of haberdashery and doyleys and lavender sachets. But now there are bag ladies. I wake up to my alarm clock, the kettle whistles, and like a Pavlov dog the vilely regulated mind or cerebral cortex that one inhabits, or vice versa, goes click and says "bag woman."

No, I say, not so, begging your pardon, making my espresso coffee, no sugar, thin china. I am a woman with a bag. I have investigated this affair and find that the people signified are actually "bag ladies" and I also find they are at the very bottom of the heap (as are we all, no matter, no matter). Bag ladies are women who search rubbish bins, equipping themselves with used plastic bags into which they insert useful throw-aways. Lately they have been searching for returnable tins of beer, price upon return threepence. Shortly ago, in the days of my husband and me, beer was served in proper glasses and the bottles were not meant for grist, no, not flung away, and not worth a farthing either, but no matter, no matter. I would not do such a thing myself but no one speaks for others. I, for one, wash the household's milk bottles. In the case of myself I am the householder, and a quarter of a pint, thank you, for the moment. These bottles are not yet disposable and one receives nothing in return. One just rinses them. This also happens in India. In the days of the tea-stations and the hoi-polloi and my husband's dear existence I was once taken to a mill-farm by the Raj, the days of the Raj being always a friend of ours, much vilified, I should say, subject to your agreement and theretofore hearing. Not to speak of comprehension and cognizance. Many things more interesting than bags themselves can come up in the course of bag-conversation.

In India, to return, I was taken to review the troops at a mill-farm. It turned out to be a milk-farm, but the bottles were certainly well rinsed. Better than in Croydon or Westminster or wherever part of the gamut you might choose. I found the same to be true in Rajasthan, Mysore, Burma, wherever the milk-farm inspections took me. A grand moment, to salute the cleanliness of milk bottles in a country with practically no cows and only a little buffalo milk that tastes of the indefatigable turnip.

To speak of myself (admitting that I know myself less well than I know many, many friends, all good to me at Church, observing my present restraint from pint milk bottles and so on owing to the economy and so on, and I therefore buying cream for the friends one has in, banging at the door all the time), I have one bag and would not use it to carry about beer cans. They are the stuff of stevedores' lunch-breaks.

My bag transports my possessions neatly. My make-up, my address book, my keys, my money, my notebook, my dark glasses, my passport, and my post office savings book, should I at any moment need to flutter them. And of course the usual letters to answer. A floating desk at the bottom of the bag, you might say, though the desk has sunk.

I have suggested to a maker of bags that they should be arranged in drawers down the side to prevent the inevitable falling and confusion. I believe the notion will bear fruit in its own time. One puts the most important things at the bottom, of course. I find there, for the record, an interestingly typed (and interesting) lecture from my son Gavin. His photograph is inside my powder compact, wrapped in cellophane. A twenty-three-year-old only, but already at the height of his powers. He tells me that the address of All Souls' College will always find him. He went to Oxford, as I know from the many postcards he sent me, and he is now a distinguished Fellow, as I can see from the lecture he sent me. As a small child he had a tendency to tail off in his thoughts but life has made him terse, as I can see from his silences in my post-box. He is undoubtedly reflective and I am sure he misses his father. His father's nature was hot-headed and not at all rambling. I am glad, most glad, that he has done so well, realising as one does that people do best *in absentia*. But I miss him.

So I present his lecture, as sent to me:

Ladies and Gentlemen, Fellows;
I was in the Second World War in the Signals Division in a

171

tent, and I suddenly saw that Eisenhower was there too, planning a campaign with another high-up, more or less. He was pointing to a map with the tip of a pair of glasses and said "We've got some stuff here, you see, and more stuff there." I thought that 'stuff' would be ammunition but it turned out to be men. Of course ammunition required men then, before this talk of the Third World War. Men-free guided missiles to kill, like food-free food. I believe I had shell-shock soon after but so did most people. At any rate I moved out of the tent.

I have been asked to deliver a lecture on the mails. In the speech of custom, deliver would often relate to a message and would entail the carrying of a message by a postman, or by a boy from the telegram office. This method is now extinct. The telegram is accomplished by exerting an insistent purchase upon the telephonic rockface of English-speaking society. Its form now takes the shape of an envelope, raising hopes, but slotted on the surface in the manner of a bill, lowering them. It arrives with less speed than correspondence in the times when sand was used to blot a letter and the letter handed to a man with a fast horse. In the days when London was working at its finest, any horse would have been linked to a gig. Not, of course, to a brougham. One finds few people who know how to pronounce either word now. A gig with a softened opening 'g' becomes a dance. A brougham, properly pronounced, has become a besom: a type of hard-faced broom. That word presents its own difficulties among the English-speaking American peoples who find it possible to remark upon a Briddish accent, which could include Tasmanian or Welsh. This is not the fault of the Raj. The Raj is blamed for too much, far too much, including tarantulas coming up the bath pipes. However,

The lecture ends here, and All Souls' College does not find him. After "tarantula" he would certainly have had something to say. He always concluded with something fresh, some clear report born of a clear mind. I believe he must have omitted several pages from the lecture. His secretary sent it to me with a memo note headed "From the desk of Lydia Nevis." I knew, of course, who she was, and that my son must have been busy or perhaps abroad, but it was startling to hear from a desk.

I do not believe that Lydia has a sense of the ordinary. At any rate, I have no evidence to the contrary. She signed herself "Lydia" with a heavy full stop after it and a line underneath it. It seemed to me more important to get my son's lecture put together in full for me. There must have been more, wouldn't you say?

Well, thinking back as one does, for all the intrusions of the many, many friends and the vicar and the health visitor who drop in for sponge cakes and pretend to lead me in directions I find frenetic—church counsel, low blood pressure, changing my bag (crocodile)—yes, indeed, the secretary Lydia is at fault in the business of the promised truncated lecture.

For my part, I want to say that I am not a bag lady. I shall undoubtedly change the contents of my crocodile bag. I have several others, stacked in the top of my cupboard. Stacked in the manner of folders; the folders are on proceeding shelves, so to speak. Having found myself, as we say in French, pursued and surrounded and robbed of the perfectly replaceable things in this bag, I shall transfer my belongings to another bag and go out with the one stuffed with beer cans. Many a try succeeds best in solitude. I shall also put into this dispensable bag a set of photographs of famous non-entities looking at salmon they have caught or admiring each other at amateur theatricals. Erstwhile friends of mine. Rich spongers who every now and then forked out for dinner. Not up to snuff.

Robbers took the air ticket I had to go to Budapest. Now that I have the replacement I shall leave tomorrow. There is no question of it. Two hours check-in time before leaving in case people want to say goodbye to their relations. For my part I very much want to hear Hungarian music again, and then I shall go to Prague, for the same reason and more. My son, like myself, must be on the move all the time to find a desk that will write for him. He said a while ago that he wants to pay my telephone bill. Or rather, his desk, Lydia's desk, says so. I prefer letters, particularly when finished, but he is not a finisher. One feels quite violently about letters ending "Dictated but not signed." The violence fades, of course, by morning.

Tomorrow will be splendid, and many years to come, if we can deal with the bomb. Not a matter of touch-wood, I think. More a matter of holding one's hush and keeping a balance. For these lessons I should greatly like to go to China, having been born there. I wonder about our missionary schools. Whether they hung on. I am sure of it. Christianity was the wrong thing for us to bring to China but China has been patient with errant mishaps for many a millennium. There, memories would be soft. They were always soft when I taught there. Softer now. There is always more. China was considered to have made a blunder, and so was the United States, and Soviet Russia, and De Gaulle's Free France, but many a blunder has a good echo.

So I sign myself, though not wishing to be personal,

Joanna Winchester,
Justice of the Peace, 1942–

About the Author

PENELOPE GILLIATT was born in London and brought up in
Northumberland. She was educated at Queen's College,
London, and at Bennington College, Vermont. She has writ-
ten four novels, four previous collections of short stories,
film criticism, the libretto for a three-act opera for the Eng-
lish National Opera, and the award-winning screenplay for
Sunday Bloody Sunday. A frequent contributor to *The New
Yorker*, she divides her time between London and New
York.